In Care of
Cassie
Tucker

YEARLING BOOKS are designed especially to entertain and enlighten young people. Patricia Reilly Giff, consultant to this series, received her bachelor's degree from Marymount College and a master's degree in history from St. John's University. She holds a Professional Diploma in Reading and a Doctorate of Humane Letters from Hofstra University. She was a teacher and reading consultant for many years, and is the author of numerous books for young readers.

In Care of
Cassie
Tucker

Ivy Ruckman

A Yearling Book

Published by
Dell Yearling
an imprint of
Random House Children's Books
a division of Random House, Inc.
1540 Broadway
New York, New York 10036

The trademarks Yearling® and Dell® are registered in the U.S. Patent and Trademark Office and in other countries.

Visit us on the Web! www.randomhouse.com/kids

Educators and librarians, for a variety of teaching tools, visit us at www.randomhouse.com/teachers

ISBN 0-440-41406-7

Reprinted by arrangement with Delacorte Press

Printed in the United States of America

April 2000

10 9 8 7 6 5 4 3 2 1

OPM

For Hillary Lynn Thalmann,
my granddaughter

Dear Diary,

My name is Cassandra Evangeline Tucker. Today is the first day of the twentieth century and I'm about to turn twelve. What could be better?

Cassie Tucker
January 1, 1900

In Cassie Tucker's words:

When school let out in the spring of 1899, my favorite teacher, Miss Deffenbach, suggested we keep a journal of the remaining months of the century.

"Someday," she said, nodding wisely, "you'll be glad you did."

A *journal*! The idea was about as appealing as castor oil. What would we write about—the weather? Whose bull chased *whom*? So far as I know, none of us bothered.

But I, Cassie Tucker, have lived to regret it. I didn't begin keeping a diary until New Year's Day of 1900. What a pity I didn't listen to my teacher. Those last few months of the century were the most exciting of my life.

Now, years later, having become the writer Miss Deffenbach predicted I'd be, I'm forced to reconstruct events and feelings from memory. But I do have a date on which everything important hinges: August 17, 1899. That day was a Thursday, and so ordinary that any journal I'd have kept then would have yawned at my jottings.

Up until dusk, that is. That's when the out-of-breath messenger from Blue Hill, Nebraska, came riding up to our gate with news that was both tragic and thrilling. We Tuckers wouldn't have to wait for the much-heralded turn of the century. The person destined to change our lives (and provide me with a story) was heading toward us that very night.

Chapter 1

"Cassie! Mama!" my younger brother, John, screamed as he flew up onto the porch. "He's after me again!"

Mama leaped up from her porch chair, spilling green beans and flapping her apron like a bullfighter. "Git, shoo! Get outa here, you mean thing!"

Our fiercest rooster pulled himself up with a bloodcurdling squawk, kicked up a whorl of dust, then hightailed it back to his hens. He knew better than to tangle with Mama.

I hustled John inside, rescuing both him and his bucket of eggs.

"Why don't we just eat 'im, Cassie?" John cried.

"That's exactly what we'll do! We'll tell Papa, and that ol' bully will get his neck wrung!"

"Yeah." John sniffled, wiping his face on my apron. "An' I'll be glad."

I held him close. He was still trembling.

"Look over here," I said in a minute. "Look what *I* just found."

I turned him around and showed him the slate I'd laid on the kitchen table. "It was in Mama's trunk. This was her slate when she was little and starting school. Like you."

I helped settle him onto the bench, then slid in from the other side until we touched.

John looked up in amazement. "There's still writing on it."

"That's my handwriting, you goose."

"All those words? What's it say?"

" 'My name is Cassandra Evangeline Tucker,' " I read. " 'I'll be twelve January eleventh, after the twentieth century arrives.' " I pointed to a chalky place where I'd erased. "See? I wrote 'nineteenth century' first because I'm so used to it. That was a mistake."

"Oh." And he began swinging his legs.

For days I'd been promising to help John write his numbers. "The first cool spell," I'd say, hoping we'd have one pretty soon. So far, the heat was bearable only in the springhouse, where I churned butter and sneaked time to read. Six-year-old John was *not* invited there.

But that afternoon a breeze was blowing in off

the Little Blue River. It brought autumn smells—wheat stubble and dusty fields—and hence thoughts of beloved school starting again.

"I think we should work on your numbers while we have a chance." I fished for the chalk in my pocket. "You need to get your nines going the other way so kids won't laugh at you."

"I hate nines!"

"You hate that rooster worse! But look what *you* get to do."

I showed him how to spit on the slate so it would polish up black and shiny. He took to that in a hurry.

When Mama started humming "Jesus, Lover of My Soul," we looked at each other and grinned. Humming meant she'd be in that porch chair a good long time.

"Here, now," I told him after he'd used his tongue on all the corners, "see if you can make a nice *1899* and a nice *1900* before Mama finishes poppin' beans."

One knuckle at a time, John got a satisfactory grip on the chalk. He was soon hunched over the slate, pressing out a long, squiggly 1.

"Good work!" he praised himself shamelessly.

I had to smile. Most of the time I loved John. I was the one who had tended him after Mama took to her bed with the crippling rheumatism. Once in a while, still, he'd slip and call me Mama.

I stood to set the table around him.

"When I get to be a real teacher," I announced to the world at large, "you, John Tucker, will be my star pupil!"

I brought plates from the tall cupboard, Papa's and Mama's first, the only ones that matched. Our older brother, Ted, although seventeen, still favored the one with a four-masted schooner. His went straight across from where John was squeaking along with the chalk.

Impishly I wondered if the world would come to an end if I switched plates around. No, better not. Mama couldn't abide such nonsense.

I leaned over John's shoulder and guided his hand for the first nine. When he insisted on doing the second one himself, I went back to counting out knives and forks. If I hurried, I could cut some pretty pink cosmos for a centerpiece.

Before long, the green beans were bubbling away in a pot as black as the stove, John had conquered his nines, and Mama had me stirring up corn bread for supper.

"Don't dawdle," Mama said now, lifting a lid to add cobs. "Fire's about ready."

I smacked the pan on the table to even the batter, then slid it into the hot oven.

John, who'd been tugging on my skirt, declared he was liking the new "cent'ry" better and better. "Zeroes are easy!" He was making circles with thumbs and forefingers, peering at the ceiling, then at me. Suddenly he twisted around and zeroed in on Mama. "Two—scary—eyes! Starin' at you!"

"The big, bad—*woof!*" Mama went after him, her misshapen hands snapping like wolf jaws. John slid squealing under the table, and Mama laughed until her face turned pink.

I loved it when she got to acting silly, like then, but it never lasted long enough. The next second she had her back to me and was motioning to have her apron tied. "The only eyes staring at us are out there in the corral," she said pointedly.

"I know, I'm going." I pulled her waist in like a calendar girl's.

"Don't use up the chalk," I called to John as I plunged on out of the kitchen. I forgot and let the screen door slam, but for once Mama didn't holler for me to come back and do it proper.

A pail in each hand, I skipped toward the barn, where our black-and-white dog would have all four milk cows rounded up. Sideways Sam—so named because he ran funny—came crawling under the bottom strand of the fence to meet me, his tail making little explosions in the dust.

The poor thing didn't get so much as a pat. I was too busy scribing circles in the air. One pail first, then the other.

"Around and around the world I'll go"—I sang to my own tune—"and where I'll stop, nobody'll know."

I'd become a teacher, for sure, if it meant I could get out of the milking.

What I didn't know that long-ago Thursday as I pressed my cheek against Maude and sent milk pinging into the pail was that everything was about

5

to change. We Tuckers wouldn't have to wait for the twentieth century, the much-ballyhooed calendar date that—according to some—signaled the end of the world.

"Unbeknownst to us all," as Papa might have said from the pulpit, the person destined to change our lives was that moment on his way to our Little Blue River farm.

Chapter 2

From the first rooster crow all the way to polishing lamp chimneys, that Thursday—August 17, 1899—had been as ordinary as dishwater.

Mama had been up since five. As usual, she was in the garden for vegetables before six. Papa, too, was up with the chickens and had the team hitched to the wagon by first light. He and Ted were headed for the town of Blue Hill by the time I'd finished dressing.

Old Mr. Pavlicek had promised Papa's country church his Swiss-made organ. Now that the old man was dead and buried, it was up to the preacher to haul it.

Upstairs, I pulled on my everyday blue-and-white

gingham and a pair of clean bloomers. John, in the narrow bed next to mine, was still in dreamland with his mouth agape.

After breakfast and prayers, it was up to John to feed and water our hundred-and-some white leghorn chickens. Like always, I did the milking—carrying two frothy pailfuls to the springhouse to cool, slopping pigs with the rest. We both weeded the garden and picked potato bugs. We had no reason to think anything was going to be different.

It was well past noon when Ted and Papa got back after moving the organ. With everyone starving, we sat right down to rabbit stew and plum cobbler, our big meal of the day. Cawky, John's sleek black crow, kept us laughing as he flapped noisily between cupboard top and John's shoulder, looking for a handout.

As usual, Papa swatted him away with "Get outa here, Nevermore!" (At least Nevermore was a nicer name than Bad News, what Queenie called him when she came to help.)

Papa had no sooner gone to the church to meet the new organist than Ted was at the pump, splashing his face and dudifying himself.

"Hold it, Cassie," he yelled as I was about to leave for the Scritsmiers'. "I'll ride you over."

Mama was sending me to pick end-of-crop beans at the next farm. Ted was going for another reason, I figured. He was hoping to see Mary Cunningham, their new hired girl from Hastings.

Well, *I* was hoping to see twelve-year-old Ruth, my best friend at school. My best friend in the Blue

Hill Township. In the whole state of Nebraska, for that matter!

But Ruthie wasn't home. She'd gone to her grandma's.

Once Mary joined us working down the rows of beans, Ted's freckled face went red as a ripe watermelon. And stayed that way. They were sweet on each other, all right, but my shy brother hardly said ten words the whole time.

Home again, I found Mama's old school slate and helped John straighten out his nines.

Life was surely uneventful for Preacher Tucker's family that third Thursday of August.

Until nightfall.

Ted wasn't home when we got the news. He had ridden back to the Scritsmiers' in a fever, to see the mustangs drovers were bringing in—he said!

"More likely to be sparking Mary," muttered Papa, who never missed a chance to tease.

Ted's face had reddened all over again, but the ribbing hadn't stopped him. He'd just swung his long legs over the end of the bench, thanked Mama for such a good supper and took off.

"I made the delicious corn bread!" I had bellowed after him.

Awkwardly, Mama lifted her coffee with the heels of her hands, as she had to sometimes. Her eyes met Papa's at the far end of the table. "They're too young to be thinking that way."

Papa cleared his throat.

I speared another bean, listening for all I was worth.

"We were too young, too," Mama mumbled, "truth be known."

"When was that?" John wanted to know, making me choke.

Then—dishes washed, lamps filled and ready—we all went outside to cool off.

Right away I thought of the Scritsmiers' tall house, where the porch is a fancy wraparound affair and the blue railings are slick as goose grease. Our back porch is pure ugly by comparison. Low-slung and splintery, it's the place we keep washtubs, mops, pails and a coffee grinder Papa was given as a marrying fee.

That night Mama claimed the rocking chair. Papa perched on the steps. John was down in the dirt with a stick. He was chattering away, demonstrating how he could write *1899* and *1900*. I sat dangling my legs and bare feet over the edge, only half listening when Mama asked about the trip to town.

I was off in my own thoughts until Papa got both hands going over the subject that riles him most. Then you can't help but listen.

"It's not President McKinley," he insisted, "it's the railroads. And those fool rumors! Mark my words, Rachel, we'll be stringing barbwire around our stock tanks. That, or be overrun."

"Hmm," Mama said, and stared off toward the river.

"The Sommerfelds are adding a wing to their boardinghouse even as we speak."

"Wish I'd gone with you." Mama rolled the hem

of her apron above her knees, then smoothed everything flat again.

I looked away. I didn't ever want to be the kind of workhorse she'd become, forever making do with her dark calico dresses and sturdy shoes. Women in town stepped out in their shirtwaists and rustly skirts, trailing their stylish boas. Not Mama!

What good was it to have hair the color of sunshine if you pulled it straight back from your temples? Sometimes I thought she didn't want to look pretty. Oh, well. No one else seemed to mind, least of all Papa, who went right on lambasting the rich Easterners and foreigners for carving up Nebraska.

I swatted a pesky mosquito and stared off, having heard it all before. Besides, a puff of dust on the river road had caught my eye, a puff now billowing into a cloud.

Seconds later, I made out it was a horse and rider. And they were turning in at the bottom of our lane.

"Papa, look there!" I pointed. "Is it Ted?"

Papa pulled up his suspenders. People come for a preacher night and day; it could have been anyone.

He struck out along the path, rolling down and buttoning his sleeves. John and I trotted at his heels.

"Can't tell who it is," he called back, "but Ted wouldn't whup a horse like that."

The rider, buckskin vest flapping, reined up sharply when he saw us. Although it was dusk, it was easy to recognize the shiny flanks of a horse run too long.

"Looking for Isaac Tucker!" The young man was blowing so hard, it was some trouble understanding him.

"I'm Ike Tucker."

"Telegram for you, sir. Come in at the Blue Hill Depot."

Papa swung open the gate.

Mama, with her hobbling walk, finally caught up with us.

"Go quick, Cassie!" She turned me around by the shoulders. "Fetch him some water."

The rider pulled off his cap. "Much obliged," he panted.

I ran as fast as my legs would carry me. By the time I got back, water had sloshed all down my pinafore. And they'd already read the telegram.

Something was wrong. John was acting strange, clinging to Mama's skirts as he hadn't for years, and the robust color had drained from Papa's face.

My own heart wouldn't stop pounding. Getting a telegram was as good as having the Pony Express ride up in the olden days, wasn't it? Still, I knew something terrible had happened.

Once messenger and horse had spun away, Mama let me see for myself. The words were hand-printed, large, on plain paper.

JOHN AND IRIS TUCKER
DEAD OF CHOLERA
HOUSE BURNED BY NEIGHBORS
SON EVAN ARRIVING THURSDAY

John and Iris? Evan! Papa's kin out West. "Dead of cholera" I understood, but what did "House burned by neighbors" mean? How awful! Who would do such a thing?

Leaving Papa at the gate, Mama pulled us back along the path, halfway toting John. She explained that Evan was our cousin. He lived out West in Montana. We'd never met him or his parents, who were our aunt and uncle.

"You mean, *Uncle* John?" I gasped. "Papa's little brother? The one he calls a heathen?"

"Yes, Cassie."

"Oh no!" He'd become a legend to us. Papa told first-rate tales about their orneriness as preacher's kids—toppling outhouses, setting haystacks afire, raiding a poor old widow's watermelon patch. Again and again we begged Papa to tell us another Uncle John story.

"Still," Mama hurried to explain, "believer or not, he was your Papa's favorite, and we named our John after him."

The idea of an unknown cousin frightened as well as thrilled me. But I knew by Mama's face as she ordered us to bed that this was not the time to ask questions.

John ran on upstairs. I stayed in the kitchen long enough to light a lamp. Pressing my face into the screen, I could see Mama going back down the path.

Papa was standing right where we'd left him.

Chapter 3

John and I began to whisper as soon as we were upstairs.

"Where do you think he is? This very minute?" I blew out the lamp. "Evan Tucker. I like his name, don't you?"

Vigorously John fanned away the kerosene fumes. "But, Cassie—does the telegram mean he's coming *next* Thursday?"

"No, goosie. He must have thought he'd be here today. He's just late. After all, he's coming from very far away. Montana's bigger than Nebraska, an' miles from where we live."

"Farther than Blue Hill?"

"Oh, much farther. A hundred times."

"Farther than Hastings on the train?"

I knew he'd just keep on, so I quit answering.

We pulled our nightclothes on in the dark so we wouldn't see each other. Plumping our pillows, we bumped bottoms and giggled in spite of everything.

"Oh, John, wouldn't it be awful?" I sobered fast as I thought what even one death would mean to our little circle. It was my worst fear, that cholera or smallpox or snakebite would take one of us. It would be John, likely, or me, since we were the youngest.

Death was Mama's worst fear, too, having lost family aplenty crossing the plains as a girl. "Nebraska was never intended for the faint of heart," she'd say when telling us about prairie fires and grasshopper plagues.

But these are modern times, I reminded myself, peering out to see if there was a moon. John and I still loved playing covered wagons, but pioneer hardships were long gone.

I sat down on my bed, taking my time brushing off my feet. Why, according to Papa, people in Blue Hill were already buying the new cream separators, and any number of folks had gone to gas lighting. Ruth and I spent hours staring at pictures of E-Z Flush Miracle Plumbing in the catalog, now that the Scritsmiers were talking about an indoor commode. With sewing machines that ran by themselves and all that talk of telephones coming . . . Well! A person could get goose bumps on top of goose bumps living in such an advanced age.

I crawled into the familiar smell of my own bedclothes. I said my prayers, mentioning Cousin Evan for a special looking-after.

"John?" I whispered when it occurred to me. "He's an orphan now, plain and simple."

John's bed squeaked as he rolled against the eaves and clamped his hands over his ears. I was scaring him.

No matter, I couldn't stop wondering how it would feel to be without a family. I knew nothing about orphans until fifteen were shipped into Nebraska on the Orphan Train, all the way from New York City. I had begged Papa for a sister then. He'd said he couldn't afford the kids he had.

Outside on the porch, Papa and Mama were still talking in low voices. They sat there a long time after we'd gone to bed, likely waiting to tell Ted. I could picture them side by side on the top step, Mama with her arms around Papa. They'd sit and talk until the moon came up.

Later on, still fighting sleep, I heard the oddest sounds drifting up through the grated register in the floor. I raised onto an elbow to listen, then fell back and covered my head with the pillow.

Papa was, finally, crying his tears.

Chapter 4

The next morning I was awake ahead of John. Ahead of Ted, too, whose room was on the other side of the stairs.

I stood at the narrow window between our beds and leaned on the sill. If I pushed my face into the screen, I could see the springhouse, its sod roof covered with dry grass and struggling buttercups.

In the other direction lay the river road, which interested me most that day. I checked the stretch of it I could see in the dim light. It was deserted. No sign of an Evan Tucker. Or anyone.

I stood there all the same, breathing in the honeysuckle and listening to the sad call of the mourning doves. Squirrels were up as well, clacking away in the top of a hackberry.

I pushed up my sleeves and let the breeze riffle the hairs on my arms. Even uppity folks in town didn't have a nicer view than John's and mine.

I got into my same blue-and-white gingham, then felt my braid to see if it was still tight. Good. Mama wouldn't have to mess with it.

Flattening on the floor, I peered down through the grate. Mama was forever telling me not to snoop, but I loved getting the first whiff of breakfast—cinnamon buns when my prayers were answered, cornmeal mush when they weren't.

Lying there, I could see that Papa had a straighter-than-usual part in his hair. I watched as he stirred cream into his coffee, then helped himself to sugar.

A shift to the right and I could see Mama breaking eggs into a skillet of sputtering grease. It had been trickiest learning to break eggs again, she'd said, after the rheumatism crippled her hands.

"We'll just tighten our belts." Mama's words drifted up as she opened the oven door.

I could smell biscuits before I ever saw them. Remembering the elderberry jelly we'd just boiled and sealed with wax, I jumped up and flew barefoot down the stairs.

"It's a judgment," Papa was saying as I came in, "plain as the nose on your face."

He reached out and grabbed me. "Cassandra, little wren, did you sleep all right?" He scrubbed my cheek with his bushy mustache.

I wriggled away with an "I guess" and slid in at my place.

After dishing up Papa's eggs, Mama broke more into the fry pan. She popped on a lid, then sat down herself.

"Shall I call the boys?" I asked.

"Not yet," Papa said. "Let it just be us for a minute."

I reached for a biscuit, but he caught my hand and made me look him in the eye.

"Cassie, your cousin Evan will likely be living with us. At least for a while. You must learn to love him as a brother. Can you do that?"

I nodded. The whole time I was thinking, *Oh, please, not another brother! Can't he just be a cousin?*

"Is he coming on the train?" was what I finally asked.

"We don't think so," Mama answered. "The telegram would have said." After studying my face a minute, she slid her cup toward me. I took a sip of coffee, slid it back. When she smiled, I realized this was a genuine grown-up talk we were having.

"How old is he, anyway?"

I also wanted to know if he was fair, like Mama, or dark like Papa's side. Was he nice? Or was he a mischief maker like Uncle John? And where in the world was he going to sleep?

Most of all, I wanted to know if heathens and infidels—people who didn't believe what we did— knew how to milk cows.

"He's somewhere between you and Ted," Papa said, "if my recollection is right."

For a while, then, we stopped talking to eat. I opened a biscuit and let the steam spiral out. I looked at Papa once, but his face was so sad I kept quiet.

"Rachel," he said later, mopping up egg with a biscuit, "did you ever find that postcard? What we were talking about?"

Mama hobbled across the dining room and into the parlor. When I heard the drawer of the library table squeak open, I remembered the faded angel card. I'd copied it once for school.

" 'Brother and Family,' " Papa read aloud to us, his hands trembling. " 'Younguns are fine and so are we. Breaking up this high prairie is worse than digging to China. Crops fail before they ever come up. Will either join the circus or go back to Indiana.' "

Papa's tears welled up. "Oh, John . . ." He shook his head. "Always the clown. Either would have been better."

He handed the postcard to Mama, who handed it to me. The pinched handwriting, strangely, looked a little like my own.

Outside, Sideways Sam was scratching fleas, his hind leg thumping the porch. Cawky would be strutting nearby, I knew, daring Sam to come ruffle his feathers. But nothing seemed funny that morning.

I was glad when the boys came down and talk turned to the hay raking Papa and Ted would be doing that day for Harley Rozendal, a neighbor with pleurisy.

John—funny little John—brightly announced

that he'd share everything with Evan: his bed, the slick bamboo pole he called Sticky, even his pet crow. "If he'd just hurry up and get here!" he said, wriggling with six-year-old impatience.

Later that morning I caught Mama using a hot curling iron on the short hairs around her face. She was primping!

"Mama, you look beautiful!" I cried, wishing she'd do mine, too.

"Well, when you know someone's coming but you don't know when, you're not good for much!" She blushed saying it, but it wasn't quite true. She'd already set eight loaves of bread to rise and made raspberry tarts.

What I wanted most that day was time to be alone so I could think about things. I also had to figure out how in the world I was going to tell my friend Ruth before she got word from someone else.

All morning I kept peering off down the lane. At first I had him clopping up to the gate in a fringed-top buggy, yellow wheels turning in a blur. His sister, whom the telegram had forgotten to mention, would be sitting on the seat beside him. She'd be the dainty sort, with a straw bonnet and pink parasol. Her name would be Alice.

By noon I had him arriving in a horseless carriage wearing a French motoring hat like we'd seen at the state fair. The motorcar would pull up with its engine sputtering, its horn squawking. Evan would whip off his goggles. He and his sister would step out into a blizzard of startled chickens.

When he finally did arrive, I was yards away in

the dark springhouse, churning. I was also on page forty-three of *Little Women,* reading in a shaft of sunlight that streamed in through a chink. I had all but forgotten I had a cousin.

"Cassie! Cassie!" came John's voice, yanking me away from the March family and back to the soddy. "He's come!"

I clapped the lid on the churn, where butter had formed ages before. My hands shook trying to untie the ribbons of the straw hat I wore for fear of snakes dropping through the roof.

"Hurry!" John insisted.

"Where is he?" I ducked out into bright sunlight, tossing the hat back through the door.

"At the gate, unloading!" John pulled me along. "He's got a gun, Cassie, an' twenty other things."

"He came in a farm wagon?" I gasped.

I could see that he did. I could also see that he was alone.

I grabbed John's hand, and we flew down the dusty path.

Mama was there helping unload. A bedroll, a water bag, a worn satchel, a greasy tarp and an ax lay on the ground. At the moment, Evan was up in the wagon bed, noisily dragging a wooden crate to the rear.

He jumped down, gripped it at both ends and dropped it at Mama's feet.

"I can certainly use another cast iron skillet," she said as she spied one in the crate. "Come along, Cassie, give us a hand."

I hurried to help, all the while sneaking looks at

Evan. He wasn't at all what I had expected: wrists dangling from sleeves too short, ankles bare above broken-down shoes. He was scarcely taller than I was. I doubted if he weighed as much.

There was nothing dandified about his dirty shirt and ragged Levi's jeans. He was brown as a cow pie and looked strong, even if stringy. My guess was that he'd slept in those very clothes for a month.

"Evan," Mama said as she straightened up, "this is your cousin, Cassandra. We call her Cassie. And our younger son here is John, named after your father."

"H'lo," I said. John ducked behind my skirt.

Evan nodded, then went right on pulling a tangle of harness out of the wagon.

By then I was eyeing his black-and-white Indian pony. In spite of being teamed with a common draft horse, it was obvious she had a restless spirit. She was the pinto of my dreams.

"What's that one's name?" I asked boldly.

"Name's Millie," he answered. "She's my saddle horse."

Wearily he shouldered a bag of oats and walked off toward the barn.

"Where's his saddle, then?" whispered John.

"Don't rush him, you two," scolded Mama. "His plate's filled with more than grief right now."

Once the wagon was empty, Evan drove it to the stock tank, where he set about watering and unhitching his team. The three of us went on carrying his things to the porch.

What interested Mama was a framed, bubble-glassed picture of Evan's mother, Iris—her hair piled high, a cameo at her throat.

"Oh my, so lovely," Mama murmured. "Papa always said his brother married a real lady."

The picture had been rolled inside what looked like a man's sheepskin coat. Maybe his father's. Carefully she rolled it up again.

What interested me most was a metal box with a hasp. It was chock full of books. I wanted to poke through to see if he had a copy of *Heidi,* but Mama wouldn't let me.

John, naturally, had big eyes for the Winchester rifle and a hunting knife. Emphatically, Mama ordered him not to touch either.

In the end, John half dragged Evan's scuffed leather satchel to the porch. There he collapsed, tongue out, offering the clear message that he'd done his bit.

Mama wasn't taken in. She sent him straightaway to gather eggs.

She gave me a job, too—the hot job of hoeing foxtail and ragweed out of the potato patch.

"I'll be in the kitchen heating water," she said, giving us a look. "He'll want to bathe in private."

As if we wouldn't know!

I had to go back to the springhouse first to mound the butter and set the crock in the cold spring water. After that, I was to keep John busy and not come near until she called.

It seemed hours. I could hardly stand it. I'd chopped out all the weeds crowding the potatoes and was working my way down through the beets. What could Mama and Evan be *doing* in there?

John got so sick of waiting, he went off behind the house to swing.

"Don't fall asleep," I teased as he ran off. He had once, and toppled out.

At long last, Mama was on the back porch beckoning me in.

"Where is he?" I mouthed at the screen door, pulling off the limp sunbonnet I used for weeding.

She nodded toward the parlor. "Be quiet, he's asleep. He's plumb tuckered out."

I helped Mama empty the bathwater into the hollyhocks. Then, as she mopped the kitchen, I tiptoed across the dining room toward the parlor. Where were Papa and Ted? The most exciting day of the year and they had to be off doing Mr. Rozendal's work.

The blinds had been pulled, so I waited a moment to let my eyes adjust. Sure enough, Evan was dead asleep, sprawled facedown on a bed that took up half the east wall.

A bed! How'd a bed get in the parlor?

I tiptoed closer.

Oh no, it's my bed! My hair ribbons were still dangling from a bedpost. The clothes he was wearing weren't his, either. I'd just ironed that blue work shirt of Papa's. Ted's pants, too. Hadn't he brought clothes of his own in that satchel?

I caught myself scowling. I hated seeing a . . . a total stranger in my bed. I wanted to run and confront Mama, but I couldn't pull myself away. For some reason there in the clock-ticking quiet, I was mesmerized by every breath he took.

I leaned closer. I sniffed at him, at his hair and his clothes. He smelled like the lavender Mama put in the last batch of soap. His skin, I could see, was as smooth as a girl's. Oh, why couldn't he have been a girl? Evelyn. Or Eva. Or Evangeline.

The thought startled me: *Evangeline, my middle name.* My word, his name was right there in the first four letters of my own. How odd!

"Cassie, whatever are you doing?" came Mama's voice.

I jumped and backed away.

"I'm just"—heat rose in my cheeks—"I'm just getting used to him."

Quickly I pushed past her and went out to find John. Even *I* didn't know what I was doing, staring so intently at my cousin.

Chapter 5

It was past suppertime Friday night when Mama stationed John and me outside. Our job was to keep Papa and Ted from waking up our cousin when they came home. It was another long wait, bordering on forever.

No sooner had John spotted the horses, their heads bobbing along above the sorghum, than we ran pell-mell down the path.

"He's here!" John shrieked, flapping both hands at once.

Papa tossed the reins to Ted and jumped off the wagon.

"An' he's plumb tuckered out," John added like a town crier.

Ted drove Doug and Barney on into the side yard. Papa made a beeline for the house.

Mama met us at the door, warning, "Shhh! All of you!"

"But, Rachel," Papa objected, "won't he be starving?"

"No, he won't. You let him sleep, Isaac Tucker!"

Mama was a sight to behold when she stood by her guns, but she did tell Papa that Evan had put away a plate of scrapple and a jug of buttermilk. "And could barely keep his eyes open doing it."

All the same, Papa crept into the parlor to have a look at the nephew he'd never seen. When he came out again, there were streaks on his cheeks. He hauled out his red handkerchief and mopped his face.

"He's the picture of John," he managed to say.

Mama cried, "Oh, Ike!" and they stood there in each other's arms, rocking from side to side.

Ted, who couldn't stand what he called displays, left to go back to the pump and wash up. John, all eyes, didn't know what to make of such behavior, either.

"It means they're happy he's here." I whispered, and lifted him onto the bench, surprised that he'd let me.

I then got real busy spooning mashed potatoes into a serving bowl. Secretly I was hoping we'd forget and make so much noise we'd wake Evan after all.

We talked of little else at the table that night.

"I plied him with questions aplenty," Mama began, once we'd filled our plates. "Prepare yourself, Ike." She looked down the length of the table. "His story's heartbreaking."

Uncle John, she said, had lost their homestead during the drought of the mid-nineties, then had moved his family all over Montana trying to keep food on the table. He'd worked at mining, lumbering, even tried sheepherding for a while.

"He was never one to stay put," Papa said quietly.

"But listen to this," Mama continued. "They had two younger children, a boy and a girl, who died in that smallpox epidemic. Poor Iris! Evan said she nearly lost her mind.

"Last summer your brother answered an ad for a farmhand and they settled in some little town on the eastern plains. He'd got in with an up-and-coming farmer who was planting red wheat from Russia. The big talk"—Mama rolled her eyes—"the big talk was that 'new seed sown in a new century' would make them all rich.

"They managed to rent a place cheap. Evan was back in school. His ma, he said, was planning her garden. Things were finally . . ." Mama looked down. Abruptly she covered her mouth.

"Then the cholera?" Papa finished for her.

She nodded, then wiped her face with her apron. "Early in May. If only . . . But it was the second scourge that year. Evan said panic raced through that town like wildfire. People jumped in their wagons and buggies and just took off. Stores closed. Streets emptied out. Only the saloon stayed open."

Mama's voice suddenly turned sharp as needle grass. "Evan couldn't get a soul to come help. Not even the preacher, Ike! He left along with all his God-fearing parishioners. John and Iris—they died within a day of each other."

Papa stared at Mama, unbelieving.

I sat there feeling I might just explode. When I heard a choking sound next to me, I reached for John, who hid his face in my lap.

"There was some old fellow"—Mama plunged on as if to get it all out at once—"your brother had helped him doctor a sick mule. He offered a corner of his land. Together he and Evan made a quick burial. Oh, Ike," Mama cried, "they're in someone's pasture! In unmarked graves!"

Papa's fist thundered onto the table, rattling plates and looping a fork into the air. "In the name of heaven, what kind of people are they up there? Who'd be so cowardly? Someone should have helped that boy! You would have, Rachel. Gone right in there! So would I!"

John's head came up. "Me too. I'd've brung 'em soup."

"Please . . . Excuse me," came a voice from the other room.

Papa, all of us, wheeled around.

"Someone did try to help."

It was Evan, standing in the parlor doorway, one hand gripping the doorjamb. He looked thin as a reed in those ill-fitting clothes. Pale, too. Had he brought the dreaded cholera with him?

Brought it right into my bed?

Papa leaped up so fast his chair smacked the floor. He was at Evan's side in seconds, helping him across the dining room and into the kitchen. Ted, too, was up, clearing the place next to him.

"Someone did try to help," Evan insisted in a voice still mushy from sleep, "but too late to do them any good." He dropped onto the bench beside Ted and across from me.

Mama poured him a steaming cup of coffee at the stove.

"Drink first," she said like a mother. "Don't talk till you're good and ready."

Evan nodded his thanks, then blew across the coffee and took a careful sip.

I stared at my food, letting gravy out of its mashed-potato dam, so that I wouldn't be staring at *him*. Ted brought utensils and a plate, which Mama began filling at once. Papa continued standing behind Evan, affectionately squeezing his shoulders. (And composing himself, I decided by the look on his face.)

"We'll rest easier," Papa said, "now that you're here with us."

Gradually Evan's color started back. His eyes, I noticed for the first time, were blue as Nebraska skies—like John's and mine. His hair was a lighter shade than I'd thought, too, with the dirt from the trail washed out.

"It was my teacher," he said as he set down his cup. "Miss Hallie. Once she got word they were going to burn the house."

"Why'd they do that?" I blurted out.

31

"Were you still in it?" squeaked John.

Papa shushed us, though Evan himself grinned for the first time. "They weren't after me," he said, speaking to John. "Not exactly."

"They were afraid the cholera would spread," Papa hurried to explain. "It's deadly, son, and people panic. They don't know how to stop the disease, so they burn house, furniture—everything!—to the ground. It's been done other places, though not much around here." He nodded for Evan to go on.

"They gave me an hour to leave town, the ones who'd stayed behind. So I packed what I could—"

He stopped talking to have more coffee, and it occurred to me that our kitchen had never been so silent.

"You see," he went on in a stronger voice, "Pa had just traded for a better team, so I hitched his matched grays to the wagon an' tied my saddle horse on behind." I could see by his eyes that he was reliving everything. "Loaded up oats, victuals, gear. And came on."

"But your teacher," Mama said as she slid Evan's supper into the warming oven, "couldn't she stop them?"

"Well, you see, Miss Hallie didn't spot my campfire until dark. I wanted to stay close, so I hobbled the horses on a little knoll right there above town. Wanted to see if they'd *really* do it."

"His father all over again!" mumbled Papa.

"I guess Miss Hallie couldn't stand it. She told me she marched into that smelly saloon and shamed

32

near sixteen dollars out of 'those drunken fools.' That's how she put it. Collected it in her bonnet."

"God bless her!" cried Papa.

"She reckoned on that being me up there. So she rode on out. The cholera didn't scare *her*. She also brought six loaves of her own bread tied up in a pillowcase. That an' some dried apples was what kept me goin' for a while."

"When'd you start shootin' jackrabbits?" Ted ventured to ask.

Evan grinned. "I shot up the whole countryside before I hit one. But I got by. Fried up a few prairie chickens, and one tough old sage hen I mostly spit out."

Listening to Evan's talk, Papa's eyes filled all over again.

"It's a miracle you ever found us!" exclaimed Mama.

"I'd told Miss Hallie earlier where I had to get to," Evan went on. "So she'd asked Chic Morton at the post office to draw me a map—likeliest way to the closest cattle trail. From there I went on to Alliance, then Ogallala. Night before last I was camped near Mormon Island on the Platte."

Papa nodded as if following him on a map.

"Never got lost till I reached Hastings. Had to sleep on the college grounds." He chuckled. "I didn't realize it till morning. Anyway, it was a straight shot to Spring Ranch from there."

No one spoke for a while. John had long since grabbed hold of my hand. I tried to imagine myself in Evan's shoes—cold, scared, hungry, cooking over sagebrush fires with nothing but a greasy old tarp when it rained. I'd be crying for Mama and Papa the whole time.

Then, as if the idea embarrassed him, Evan told us Miss Hallie had offered to be his guardian, let him live with her. She kept on offering, too.

"But, you know, I was ready to leave that place." He looked at Papa as if he'd understand. "I knew I could trade off a horse if I had to."

"And did you have to?" Papa asked.

"At Fort Kearny. After breaking a wheel. Pa's shotgun and my saddle went, too. In Hastings, before I got lost, I figured I'd better send a telegram while I still had money—before something else broke down. Cy Wolfe, the stationmaster there, worded it for me.

"Wolfe . . ." Evan smiled engagingly at John. "That's a funny name for a man, huh?"

John nodded earnestly.

Suddenly Evan said, "Oh, wait." Right there at the table in front of Mama and me, he began to unbutton his shirt.

All talk stopped as he reached inside and pulled out, of all things, a folded white pillowcase. A *once-* white pillowcase that was edged with purple-and-pink tatting.

"I figured you could use this, Aunt Rachel." Briefly he held it to his nose. "Still smells like Miss Hallie's bread."

Papa was so moved, he had us down from that

table in a flash, kneeling beside chairs and benches to offer up the prayer he could no longer contain.

"Miss Hallie, my Lord, what an angel!" Papa sang out to the rafters. "Sent from God! To guide and protect young Evan on the saddest journey of his life."

Papa's preacher voice filled the room, his words so strong and heartfelt they raised prickles on my arms.

"And what a time to send my brother's son, at the harvesting of a century! Another precious soul for us to raise up according to the Gospel and our own best lights."

Surprisingly, there came an "Amen!" from Ted's quiet corner. My own eyes were squeezed so tightly shut, I could no longer see the orange linings of my eyelids.

In the end, Papa's prayer came down to a whisper. There was a long pause, and then his voice went trembly with all he must have been feeling and remembering.

"I commend unto God my dear brother and his wife, Iris, whose tragic deaths have broken our hearts."

Mama had started to cry. Softly. I wished she wouldn't.

"But let us be reminded," Papa finished, "in death, as in the fullness of life, Thy will be done. Thy will be done above our own, now and forevermore. Amen."

"Amen!" echoed the rest of us.

Just in time, I thought, inhaling the smell of pork gravy that was again bubbling on the stove.

Evan himself was still seated when the rest of us rose to take our places again. He hadn't budged. Nonetheless, the praying had put a startled, wide-eyed expression on his face.

There was no trace of cholera about him now as he dived into the plate of supper Mama had fixed for him.

I slept in my own room for the last time that night—on a down comforter Mama had folded on the floor beside John.

"After this," she explained, "you'll be sleeping in your own bed, but in the parlor. The upstairs will be for the boys."

"The boys and not me? But, Mama, why?"

"Not now, Cassie. Things change, and we have to do what we can. Now go to sleep, both of you. It's been a long, hard day." She blew out the lamp and went downstairs.

I wanted to cry. I loved everything about our cozy room—its angles, its crannies, the lofty view of the world it afforded day after sunny day. I stared into the dark, burning with outrage.

How could I love someone who was stealing my room, even if he was a poor, homeless orphan?

Papa was happy as a fox in a henhouse to have Evan here with us, but who cared a bean about me?

"Don't cry, Cassie," John whispered before long. He had reached down with his foot and was patting my head. "Remember what they talked about this morning? Next summer Papa's gonna build on another room, huh?"

"Maybe," I blubbered. "Everything's maybe, don't you know that, John? *Maybe* I'll get a pony. *Maybe* I can have music lessons. *Maybe* they'll build on a room—"

Bleakly I heaved myself over against the wall. I began to think Queenie might have been right. Queenie, who read tea leaves in her gypsy wagon, who had secretly read mine one day and said she saw tribulations ahead.

Suddenly I longed for her big warm arms and motherly ways and wondered why she was so late in coming. The gypsy camp at the river stood empty—no music, no smoky campfires, no happy shouting of children.

I waited until John was asleep, then got up and stood at the window. I pushed my face hard against the screen. *Everything* was changing. I didn't like it a bit!

Chapter 6

As far away as the milking stalls, I could hear the rest of the family laughing. It was Saturday morning, and they were all outside loading the wagon for a trip to town. Twenty-two dozen eggs, a can of cream and four dressed chickens were heading for the boardinghouse in Blue Hill. Ma Sommerfeld's was one of the few places that paid cash.

The rest of the wagon would be crammed full of garden stuff—roasting ears, kohlrabi in bundles, beets and peppers in baskets.

"Trading day'll be no chore at all with Evan helping load," Pa had said at breakfast, inviting him to pick a bushel of tomatoes—a job that had been mine for years.

I finished milking Tess, set the brimming pail on the wooden bench, then moved my stool to the next stall. *No doubt he'll end up Mama's favorite as well as Papa's,* I thought. He'd told them at breakfast he wasn't afraid of work. Good thing! There was plenty of it.

I gave a yank on Bessie's teat that brought her head sharply around. "Sorry, Bessie." I patted her flank. "It's not your fault."

When I looked up again, Evan was coming in through the square of sunlight that marked the open barn door.

"Your pa said you'd show me the stock today," he announced. "Looks like they're about ready to leave."

I hated getting stuck at home because there were too many of us for the wagon. That meant that only Mama and Papa could go. I'd hoped we'd be taking Evan's rig as well, but Papa said his horses were tired and needed a shoeing.

"Why can't Ted show you?" I asked, a bit too snippy, and went on milking. Ted was the expert on livestock. Let him do it.

"He said he's going hunting with the Spitfires."

"Spitfires!" I howled. "You mean the Scritsmiers!" I laughed so hard I slid sideways off my one-legged stool. I had to get up and adjust everything again.

Evan, who was leaning over the stall like some straw boss, merely looked at me. "Know something? I'd better see a doc about my hearing. I'd a sworn your name was Sassy when I first heard it."

"Hee-haw," I brayed like a donkey. I was hardly being ladylike.

"Say, is that Blue Hill place big enough for a post office?" he asked shortly. "Spring Ranch was so piddlin', they didn't have one. I need to mail something."

"Like what?" I asked, aiming a squirt of milk at one of the barn cats.

He pulled a cameo brooch out of his pocket, the same pin I'd seen in his mother's portrait. "I want Miss Hallie to have it. You know, for all her trouble."

"Oh," I said, ashamed suddenly of my manners. "Mama will mail it for you. Go tell her."

He looked at the brooch a long time, oblivious of me, then slid it back into his pocket. He was in no hurry to leave.

"Guess what?" I said, thinking I'd cheer him up. "We might go to the Hastings Street Fair. In September. If Mama saves enough egg money. Ever been to a street fair?"

"Nope. Don't suppose you'd want a street fair where there's only one street. And that full of mud and dung."

I moved Bessie over after milking her dry, then parked myself next to Maude, whose tail swished around and caught my cheek. "Easy, Maude, it's just me."

Evan stepped out of her line of sight. I was hoping he wouldn't leave, now that we'd started talking. "So what was it like where you lived?" I hurried to ask.

He stared off at the barn door, as if he could see the whole town laid out there among the sunlit motes of dust.

"The last place we lived," he began, "the school was over the feed store. Funny place for a school, but it always had been, kids told me. Next to that there's McBride's, where you go for sugar, brooms, kerosene, an' like that."

"What else?"

"There's a Catholic church and one that isn't. And one saloon. The Cross-Eyed Goat. They paid me a nickel to sweep there sometimes. After the Saturday-night rowdies."

"You worked in a saloon?" I hooted. "So . . . are you Catholic?" I twisted against Maude so I could see his face. In shifting around, I missed the bucket and sprayed my foot.

"No," he said, looking away as if he hadn't noticed. "If you have to know, I'm not Catholic."

"That's okay. So what are you, anyway?" I asked, sounding more like John-the-persistent every minute.

He smacked a support post with his hand.

"I'm nothin'," he said, giving me a straight look.

"I never heard of 'nothing.' Everybody's something! We're United Brethren. UB for short. So what are you?" I knew full well that Uncle John's family were not churchgoers, but something made me want to goad Evan nonetheless.

"I'm nothing, I told you."

I threw him a squinty look that must have made him mad.

"Forget it. I don't chew my cud twice!" And at that he walked out of the barn.

At least, I thought, *I didn't call him a heathen to his face.* Come to think of it, I hadn't asked if he knew how to milk, either, a question uppermost in my mind.

With Ted gone hunting with Carl and Bones, Mama seemed more than happy to set out a cold lunch for those of us staying home.

"No more chores today," she'd said. I'd just come in from the springhouse, where I'd poured the milk into cooling pans. My jaw dropped. Who'd skim off the cream if I didn't?

"Take a holiday, Cassie! You needn't be so serious. Just do what's necessary. Call it Evansday, how about that? You three can get nicely acquainted while Papa and I are gone."

She'd never say such a thing—ordinarily. The "no chores" part, that is.

John himself jumped up and down, shrieking, "Thursday, Friday, Evansday! It's a holiday! Papa, bring us some candy!"

"Keep an eye on your brother," Papa called minutes later from the wagon seat. "And Evan, you feel free to nose around the farm. Can't get lost on eighty acres."

Evan didn't do much nosing around as it turned out. By late morning we were sliding down a bank on the Little Blue River, with me toting the lunch and Evan toting a jar of cold spring water. We were having ourselves a picnic!

I'd decided to wear the bib overalls a thresher had

left at our house a month before. They were way too big and ugly as could be. John had laughed his head off seeing me in men's pants, but for once I wasn't going to miss out on the fun. I'd sworn both Evan and John to secrecy. They were not to tell Mama, no matter what. She thought it the biggest sin in Christendom for a girl to wear boys' clothes.

Evan said his own ma wore Levi's on occasion. She wore his pa's big sheepskin, too, when the weather got so cold she couldn't reach the henhouse without frostbite.

"So today I'll be a Montana girl!" Suddenly feeling daring, I rolled the bottoms several more inches above my ankles. I was still more covered than pictures I'd seen of lady bathers.

The day was summer-perfect, with a sky the blue of Mama's Dutch delft teapot. The day was also plenty hot, and so still we could hear sounds of life all around—hoppers clicking in the weeds, a quail calling "Bob White," darning needles buzzing. There must have been a million little creatures darting along the riverbank.

Remembering ants, we jammed the canvas lunch bag high in the crotch of a cottonwood. We then helped John gather stones for a dam so we could store our water jar where it wouldn't get washed away.

After that, Evan couldn't wait. He stripped off his shirt, rolled his pants above his knees and waded in, more nearly naked than we Tuckers were ever allowed to be. He was laughing and up to his undershirt in seconds.

"Come on in!" he beckoned, splashing in backward. Yelling "Whoooeee!," he floated out into the current, toes up and grinning like a skunk.

I was grinning myself, but I wasn't that brave! I'd never really been *in* the Little Blue River, only wading at its edge, like John. Staring down at the moving water made me so dizzy I figured I might just topple over. Lord knows, I couldn't swim if I had to!

"John"—I swung around to warn him—"stay there where it's shallow, you hear? Build something with those pretty stones."

When I looked back again, Evan was gone. I couldn't see him anywhere. Had he floated out of sight that fast?

"Cassie!" John hollered from the bank where he'd plopped down to roll his pant legs. "Where'd Evan go? Has he drownded already?"

"Evan!" I called, searching both ways, then peered into the brush opposite. *"Evan!* Are you over there?"

The Little Blue rolled by without offering a trace—not a dimple, a bubble, nothing. I held my breath and motioned for John to be quiet. Maybe we'd hear him if we listened. I finally had to swing around to stifle John, who kept screaming "He's drownded!" at the top of his lungs.

"Evan!" I screamed again. John's panic was catching.

At that moment a red-faced Evan leaped up right in front of us. Water streamed from his hair, his face, his sagging undershirt. He gulped in the air, then burst out laughing.

"Don't *do* that!" I scolded. "You scared us to death!"

John, by then, had a good grip on my overall straps and was trying with all his might to get me back on the bank.

"Can't you swim?" Evan shouted up at me. "Come on in, it's not that swift. Hey, Cassie—" He dived under, then popped up again, like a fish leaping for air.

Show-off!

"You want to learn?" he yelled from the middle of the river. When he stood and started wading back, I could see that the water was only waist deep. Still, it was too deep for me.

"Hey, I'll teach you. You want me to?"

I must have stared dumbly at such an idea. How many times had I been here with Ted and the Scritsmiers? No one had ever said we girls might be able to swim. Girls just didn't, so far as I knew. Every time, Ruth and I would go home with our dresses soaked and muddy, braced for a good scolding. But swim? Our mamas would have us think it wasn't possible.

"Get rid of those britches," Evan said before I'd actually made up my mind. "They'll drag you down. Go on, I'll turn around. I won't look, I promise."

Quickly I got out of the overalls and my hot long-sleeved blouse, wadding them up and stuffing them in the tall grass. It made me giggle to feel so light and airy.

I slid into the river with only John peeking and felt the cool water come right through my cotton chemise and long bloomers. I crouched primly near the bank at first, dealing with a severe case of shivers. Evan finally coaxed me out a few feet.

For the next hour or so, with John busily building a horse barn out of mud and driftwood, I, Cassie Tucker, had my first swimming lesson.

Evan's method was to take me by the waist, give me a giant shove toward the bank, then holler what I should do: "Kick, kick, kick! Atta girl! Now plow with your arms!"

Pretty soon I could dog-paddle back from several yards out. I could hold my breath underwater— briefly!—and was just getting the knack of stroking.

Evan told me I was a "natural-born swimmer," that I learned way faster than he did. "With the Little Blue so close—gosh! You should have been in here swimming all along."

What was wrong with our mamas? I began to wonder. Just because they didn't know how. So far as I could tell, there was no sin in a girl's learning to swim. None whatsoever.

Papa said God made the meandering Little Blue for animals and the land. I figured He had swimmers in mind, too.

Chapter 7

By the time any of us thought about food, the sun stood at three o'clock and I had learned to swim. I'd loved the heavenly, slippery feel of the river rippling around me. I'd loved getting my long braid drenching wet so that I could squeeze it out again. It was also nice to discover I was actually good at something.

But when John set up a howl—"I'm gonna eat my lunch and yours, too!"—Evan and I decided it was time we got out.

Evan went downstream to a clump of willows while I pulled my overalls on over my sopping wet underthings. Not easy! We hadn't thought to bring a rag or a towel, and the struggle made me giggle.

"How come you're laughing like that?" John asked.

"No reason, you goose. I'm just happy." I grabbed him up and swung him around.

"Remember now," I said as I set him down, "we can't tell Mama about what I did. Someday maybe. And then, when she gets used to the idea, I'll teach you, okay?"

Evan retrieved the canvas lunch bag, and we sent John after the water jar. The overalls sticking to my limbs might truly have been embarrassing, but the boys had eyes only for the sausages and thick slices of buttered bread Mama had fixed.

John showed Evan how we wrap our bread around the meat and pickle both to make a sandwich. Then, forgetting to say grace or even *think* grace, we chomped down like pigs at a trough.

No one talked. It wasn't necessary. We'd had a perfect holiday. An Evansday for sure! I didn't want it to end.

We handed the jar around and washed down our raspberry tarts. We also had to listen—at length—to how John had built his mud-and-driftwood barn for ten wavy-tailed Percheron horses.

Moments later, Evan flopped backward into the tall prairie grass, arms spread wide. "Ooooh, I'm full as a tick," he moaned.

"I'm lazy as a pig," followed John, landing alongside Evan.

I couldn't think what I was, but I flopped down by John and we all laughed like loonies.

For the longest time we just lay there in the afternoon quiet and let the sun warm us. It was a wonder we didn't fall asleep.

"I think," John said by and by, "I think I see Iris."

I gasped and sat up. How could he say such a thing? How did he even remember her name?

"Where?" Evan asked, motioning me back. "Where do you see her?"

"Right up there"—John pointed—"in that cloud. The one with a face coming on it."

Evan lay back and shaded his eyes. "I see her, too. Plain as anything."

"Papa said she's in heaven, so I guess she is, huh?"

Evan didn't say anything, but his breath quickened. His chest, in fact, was shaking the front of his shirt. From being chilled, for sure, but maybe from something more.

"If she's anywhere," he said at last, "she's in heaven."

That satisfied John.

Some later, with clouds blocking the sun, I began to feel shivery myself. I stood to shake the crumbs out of our lunch cloth, thinking John and I should start home. Evan could stay if he liked. It would be nice for Mama if I had the table set and potatoes going for supper.

Once standing, I could hear wheels creaking, and not that far away. Tilting my head, I could also hear the clank of a doubletree. Someone was coming toward us on the river road. They weren't in a hurry. The *clop-clop, clop-clop* was slow and easy.

It was too early for Mama and Papa to be coming home. The trip to Blue Hill, with all they had to do, would take the day. Nonetheless, I nudged John with my toe. "We'd better go. I need to change clothes before . . . you know."

John let out a groan. He'd have sprawled in the sun till dark. Especially with Evan there. He rolled over and squinted up at me. "Tell us that pome you wrote," he said out of the blue.

He was stalling.

"What *pome?*" I asked, knowing full well what he wanted.

" 'I once knew a boy whose name was John,' " he began. "Go on, Cassie, tell it."

" 'Sat at his desk with his britches on,' " I said in a singsong. " 'He learned to parse and figure, he was oh so smart—' "

John jumped up to finish it himself: " 'And gave his nineteen hundreds a jolly good start!' "

Evan covered his mouth in mock horror. "Oh my, what were you doing at the desk with your britches off?"

"On!" shouted John. "He had his britches *on!*"

"Whew!" Evan rolled his eyes. "Good thing."

The wagon was nearly alongside by the time John heard the horses snorting and blowing. He bounded up to see who was coming.

I had thought we were well out of sight. Somehow, though, sharp-eyed Queenie had spotted us through the trees. I could see her, too, as she came into view, puffing ahead of the gypsy van, her fleshy brown arms waving over her head.

"Girlie-girl!" she yelled. "Yoo-hoo!"

"Oh boy, it's Queenie!" John cried. And before I could stop him, he'd clambered up the bank and was running to meet her.

"Guess what we been doin'?" he shouted to the heavens.

Oh, for a gopher hole! Telling her was like telling Mama. No difference.

Along with her scrawny husband and kids, Queenie came to live on the Little Blue every summer, both to get away from the heat in Hastings and to be part of a larger gypsy encampment. Some years she'd arrive early to help cook for threshers. This year, I figured, she'd get stuck with the canning and sewing.

By now her kids had spotted us as well. Little heads poked out of windows like so many chickens in a crate—Marie and Fay and smiley Ernestine. Roberto, my age but extremely shy, swung off a pole at the rear and waved.

Their habit was to camp at the river as long as the weather held. They'd also help themselves to our garden, our chickens, whatever they needed. Papa let them. He'd usually give them a pig besides, in exchange for Queenie's help in the house.

"Has your mama gone to town?" she said, puffing toward us in her flower-bright dress, her dozen bracelets jangling.

I grinned—sheepishly, I'm afraid—and nodded.

"And who's this young man?" She towered above us, hands parked on her hips.

Evan sat up.

"That's Evan!" John shouted. "My new brother!"

"Oh, my stars and garters!" Queenie said, sizing him up, most likely thinking, *Someone else to do for.*

"He's our cousin," I corrected John.

"Got here just in time for haying, looks to me. You staying long?"

My question exactly!

Evan hunched his shoulders. I guess he didn't know what to say.

By then, however, Queenie had turned her attention to the sight of "her Cassie" in men's overalls.

"Your mama know you're at the river? Like that?" She peered at me through the half-moons of her glasses. Her head went side to side. "Rachel's like to have a fit." She walked away with enough tongue-clucking to turn me red.

I rolled up our lunch things, latched on to John's hand and dragged him up the bank. We ran all the way home with Evan following.

"What's wrong?" John kept asking. "Queenie likes us."

Didn't he know what would happen once Queenie told Mama?

I'd just had my first—and last—swimming lesson.

Chapter 8

Queenie never got a chance to tell on me. John beat her to it. Of course, the first thing he said when Mama and Papa drove into the side yard was "Did you bring licorice?"

The second, with hardly a breath between, was "Guess who's here? Queenie!"

The rest of the details came pouring out—how funny I'd looked in the overalls and how Evan had taught me to swim. My stomach hurt already. Even before stepping down from the wagon, Mama had me fixed with her sternest look.

I was quick to mention that I'd already started greens and potatoes on the stove, knowing she'd be tired. "Want me to make a custard?" I asked. "I could, real fast."

"Cassie, go to your room!" Mama pointed with a stiff arm. "At once. There'll be no supper for you."

My eyes filled. I couldn't go to my room, didn't she know that? I didn't have a room! Evan was up there in "my room" this minute, sorting out his things.

I turned on my heel, knowing I couldn't argue, and ran back to the house. Why was Mama so mean? I had loved the day. I had loved being in the river and learning to swim.

"Mama, you big day-killer!" I said aloud as I flopped across the bed in that sticky hot parlor. I hadn't been the least bit naughty. She'd told us to take a holiday, hadn't she?

I pushed my face into the pillow, hating Mama and my tattletale brother equally.

But in spite of my being banished from the family, some things happened that Saturday night that made me feel better. Mama, who seemed a bit on the sorry side, came into the parlor after supper was cleared away. She wanted to show me the pretty new piece goods she'd bought with her egg money. The material was smooth and shiny. Chintz, she called it. The pattern was hundreds of tiny pink and yellow flowers scattered across a deep crimson background.

"What's it for?" I said with a sniffle. I was hoping she'd say, "It's for you, for a new school dress."

She didn't. She said it was for a screen.

A screen! Who wants a screen?

"Your Papa's going to nail together some tall frames. With hinges, you know? To make a folding screen. Queenie will sew this up for the panels. It'll give you some privacy. Besides, it'll look nice in the parlor."

When I didn't say anything, she dropped tiredly onto the bed.

"Cassie, you're almost twelve. A young lady your age is expected to act like a lady, even in a houseful of boys."

I stroked the smooth fabric and nodded.

"More particularly," she went on, "a young lady does not loiter at the river dressed in some disgusting remnant—like those overalls! Are you listening? She's apt to be mistaken for a railroad tramp. Or worse. It's unseemly, and I don't want to hear of your doing it again."

Hot tears stung my eyelids. I felt like asking who'd do the milking if I had to stay in my "room" forever. I didn't, of course. She'd call it sassing.

I just lay there after Mama left, staring up at a ceiling crack with the cool chintz fabric in my arms.

It was Papa who slipped in next. He told me Mama had seen a little boy drown during a baptism in that very spot on the Little Blue. I could see it saddened him to have to tell me.

"Rachel couldn't bear losing one of you children." He bent and kissed me on the nose, then whispered, "Neither could I."

Sometime later, I could hear Mama's voice and John's, shouting over checkers on the porch. Papa, too, was out there, singing "Sweet Betsy from Pike" at the top of his lungs as he set up for a chess game with Evan. Ted had quit playing chess because he never won. Papa sounded thrilled to have an opponent again.

"Cassie, you awake?" came a loud whisper from the dining room doorway.

I sat up.

"Quick, take this!"

A fried chicken leg was thrust under my nose.

By the time I realized it was Evan, he was gone.

It was my only supper, and I was starving. I smacked my lips over every juicy bite, then sucked the bone clean. Afterward I pushed it deep down inside the pillowcase. It wasn't so bad, after that, to hear everyone else having fun without me.

As a result of such kindness, Evan moved up a notch in my estimation. No longer did I wish him gone. Now, in fresh imaginings, we were both orphans and on the train together, heading for the Omaha orphanage. With Mama dead of rheumatism and Papa called to the mission field (as good as dead), we'd have to make our way in the world alone.

Of course, the Scritsmiers would come to visit us. Ruth would fall weeping on my neck because she missed me. Also Carl, Bones and the twins. They'd bring fried chicken and baked beans and an angel food cake, frosting piled high. We'd picnic along the banks of the wide Missouri and sing our sad songs.

I never knew when they lighted the lamp; never saw its glow beyond the parlor window. Papa and

Evan, I heard later, had battled it out with their chessmen until eleven that night.

Papa's "Checkmate!" was so loud it woke Mama and Ted both. I slept through it all, dreaming of swimming in the Little Blue.

Chapter 9

Papa's church, as we in the family thought of it, was a redbrick building that had started out as a four-room schoolhouse. A bell tower and vestibule had been added and the inner walls removed. A line of hitching rails ran down both sides of the building and a carriage barn was built behind. It now served as church and meeting place.

Evan didn't protest when Papa announced he'd be expected to worship with us each Sunday. I only hoped he didn't feel as miserable as he looked. Ted's old herringbone suit was plainly a size too big, but Mama wouldn't dream of sewing on the Sabbath. She'd merely pinned up the hems of the pant legs, saying, "Walk easy if you don't want to get stuck."

For the first time ever, that Sunday we were to have real organ music to accompany our singing. No more pitch pipes! Miss Margaret Warwick had already taken her place "at the console" (Papa's words) by the time we got there. Church was solemn as she rendered the first song, a full-stopped version of "For the Beauty of the Earth." I wanted to stand up and clap when she finished.

Papa began the service by thanking God for Old Mr. Pavlicek. Not in those words, of course. Mr. Pavlicek's first name, which most of us had never heard, was actually Jan, pronounced *yawn*. He had been the head of a large Czech family that had emigrated to Nebraska in the 1860s and the first for miles around to own an organ.

After an opening of four hymns (two more than usual), Papa surprised his congregation by asking how many had promised they'd pray for rain during the week. "Raise your hands," he insisted. "Let me see who you are."

I turned around. Hands were up everywhere. We all knew the corn would turn to dust if it didn't rain soon.

"So . . . ," Papa went on, nodding and biding his time. His dark eyes ranged over the sixty or so parishioners, most of whom were fanning themselves. "How many of you brought your umbrellas today?"

There was a ripple of laughter. Not one hand went up.

Ducking behind the pulpit, Papa extracted the black umbrella from home. He opened it with a snap and pumped it up and down over his head.

Mrs. Knightly, up front due to her hearing, gave a gasp that carried halfway back. "Bad luck!" she said, gripping the pew ahead with lacy gloves.

Ted whispered, "Cloudburst time!"

Evan, sitting between us, stifled a laugh.

But Papa was busy making a point. "O ye of little faith!" he scolded, his stern look seeking out the usual slackers. He collapsed the umbrella and tossed it behind him. "There won't be any rain if we don't expect rain. How can God figure out what all of us farmers are praying for if we don't believe?"

Evan bumped my elbow. He and Ted had been sharing grins, but now his approving look was for me. I don't think he'd expected church to be so— well, so interesting.

Then Anna Warwick, Margaret's younger sister, sang "Will There Be Any Stars?" There wasn't another sound as her voice rose above the organ and filled the church.

Papa started blowing his nose after the first chorus.

Then the plate went around (more organ music), and it was time for the sermon.

Papa had another surprise in store for us. After

telling Mama he was preaching his "Bringing in the Sheaves" sermon, due to the season, he up and announced a whole new topic: "What makes a Good Samaritan?" Evan's story—about his parents, himself, and the kindness of Miss Hallie—provided Papa with his material.

It was the best preaching I'd ever heard. Mama agreed. The words, she said later, came straight from the heart. He hadn't written down a single sentence beforetime.

In closing, Papa's voice rose to a pitch that sent chills up my arms: "They not only walked on the other side of the street, those folks in their panic, those good Montana brethren." He slapped the sides of the pulpit. "They—left—town!"

His eyes were ablaze as they ranged over the congregation, but his voice dropped to a whisper as he made his point with scripture: " 'Inasmuch as ye have done it unto one of the least of these, my brethren,' Jesus said, 'ye have done it unto me.'

"Let not such a thing happen here," he admonished his deeply affected congregation. "Not in the community of the Little Blue. We are our brothers' keepers!"

"Amen!" came voices from all over the room.

There was hardly a dry eye when Papa finished speaking. Evan himself sat with his head lowered, his ears afire. At the end, when Papa asked him to please stand, Ted and I very nearly had to haul him to his feet.

Miss Warwick's "Amazing Grace" was, indeed, amazing that morning. She played on and on as folks crowded forward to meet Evan, then lingered to watch her coax music out of Old Mr. Pavlicek's mahogany organ. I wondered, standing proudly beside Evan, if he now thought he'd like "being something" better than "being nothing."

Chapter 10

Before church was over, Mama got offers of hand-me-downs from two families who had boys Evan's age. In addition, Mr. McCleery, who owned the Blue Hill Mercantile, pressed a note into her hand that said, "I'd be honored to provide a new suit of clothes for your brave young man." He'd added a P.S.: "Shoes as well." He must have noticed the sorry slabs of leather Evan was wearing.

After everyone else had gone home, we gathered around the buggy to tell Papa goodbye. He was heading for Spring Ranch, where he'd preach again at an afternoon service. Since their Ladies' Aid vied over who'd get to feed him, Mama teased that he ate better on the Sabbath than the rest of us.

As usual, then, Ted took the reins. Mama sat on the wagon seat beside him. The rest of us piled in the back. We were home in twenty minutes and out of our Sunday clothes in ten more.

With Papa gone, Sunday afternoons were more or less our own. We were luckier than most preachers' kids, who weren't allowed to do anything on Sundays. No baseball, no horseshoes, no tree climbing. No real work, either, except tending to livestock. Reading and visiting were about the only acceptable pastimes.

But the Tuckers were not a sitting-around kind of family, the Scritsmiers even less so.

Mama, having served sandwiches and potato salad from the sideboard, retreated to her room and closed the door, the way she did most Sundays. *McClure's Magazine* went with her. The latest installment of *A Gentleman from Indiana* was of particular interest that day, she told us.

John, thank goodness, loved playing alone. So long as he could be a Union soldier or hunt bears with Sticky, he was happy, and he would run off to play right after eating.

"Mama?" I said that day, tapping lightly on her door. "We're going now. Evan's going over with us."

"Over," she knew, meant to the Scritsmiers'. Since our nearest neighbors were not Sabbath-keepers, Mama could hardly give us her blessing. Her silence we'd learned to take as permission.

With Evan using Papa's saddle, the boys soon had Prince and Millie cinched up and ready to go. I climbed on behind Ted, not caring that my petticoat showed, and we took off.

Ted and I led the way, cutting off across Plum Canyon, tearing over a rise, then stretching out for a good run on the flats. We arrived at the Scritsmiers' picket fence laughing and out of breath.

Oh, how I longed for a pony of my own!

Mary Cunningham saw us first and leaped up from the porch swing. I could see why Ted liked her. In her Sunday frills, framed by two white porch posts, she was pretty as a postcard. Her dark brown curls and rosy cheeks made me hate my own pale looks even more.

Seconds later Ruthie came swinging out of the house in a yellow pinafore. Carl, the oldest, and tall, lanky Bones, Ted's best friend, were right behind her.

"Hey, Ma, come see what the cat drug in!" hollered Carl.

"Where'd you git that there purty girl?" teased Bones, who always made me laugh with his goofy farmer-talk.

The twins tumbled out after them—Lena and Leon, nine-year-olds, the unkempt members of the family. The parents seemed occupied with something on the porch off the kitchen, but Mrs. Scritsmier finally looked up and waved, then started down the steps.

That was the family—six children, if you included the baby buried in the rose garden. They always did when they counted, so I did, too.

"Guess what?" cried Ruth. "We're having ice cream! Papa just started cranking."

"In August?" I squeaked.

Just then Prince, as if he'd understood *ice cream,* bobbed and nickered comically, making everyone laugh.

"It's the end of the ice," said Mrs. Scritsmier, picture-perfect in a starched and tucked shirtwaist. "The Little Blue will just have to ice over and give us more." Smiling warmly, she patted me on the knee. "How's your mother, Cassie?"

"She's fine."

Bones, who was Ted's age, made a stirrup with his hands so I could slide off Prince.

It came to me then that everyone was staring at Evan except Carl, who was circling Millie like a horse trader. I caught Ted's eye. Being so shy, he mightn't have told a soul.

"This's our cousin Evan," he said as he dismounted. "He's a Tucker, same as us. Just got here. Drove a team and wagon all the way from Montana."

"By himself!" I added.

Evan nodded at Bones, who nodded back.

Carl, having spent a summer driving cattle into Montana, was so impressed he doffed his hat. "That's mighty big country!"

"I can't believe you came all that way alone!" exclaimed Mary, favoring him with one of her blazing smiles.

Ruth couldn't take her eyes off him. I had to

poke her. Astride such a beautiful pinto, he honestly did look much improved. I was glad Mama had taken the scissors to his hair.

We didn't have his company for long, however. The boys were soon hustling him off to the corral to see the mustangs they were trying to break.

"You do any roping up there? Any bronc bustin'?" Bones asked Evan as they led him away.

"Oh, just foolin' around," came Evan's reply as the rest of us walked on to the house.

Mary went back to her embroidery on the porch swing.

Mrs. Scritsmier went back to making ice cream.

Ruth and I linked arms and headed upstairs to her room, which was a corner turret at the rear of their big farmhouse. It was a room fit for a princess. I loved being there. And to think we had the whole afternoon to ourselves. For talk, first. Paper dolls next, I hoped. We needed to make clothes for Maisie and Katrina before their first day of school.

Too excited to contain myself, I raced to get ahead of Ruth on the stairs, but she caught up and mashed me against the railing.

"I wasn't at Grandma's *that* long. Where have you been?" She grabbed my neck, pretending to choke me. "You're not going to like your cousin more than me, are you? *Are you?*"

"Evan?" I giggled. "I hate boys!" We scuffled and laughed some more.

"But"—I caught my breath—"Papa says I have to be nice to him, so I'm trying."

"I don't hate boys like I used to," she confided. "But"—in a whisper—"I don't want one for a best friend."

"Oh, me neither!"

We found a spot on the window seat overlooking the rose garden. Shouts and laughter drifted up from the corral, where there were as many horses churning around as boys.

"So, now, tell me everything," Ruth insisted, turning me around to face her. "My mama heard from your mama in town yesterday that he may be living with you." She grabbed up my hands. "Cassie, is that true?"

For once I had something wide-eyed Ruth Scritsmier didn't—an orphaned cousin. I smiled happily and started in.

What I didn't know, painstakingly covering every detail of the past four days, was how disastrously that Sunday afternoon was going to end.

Chapter 11

After two hours of wrangling wild horses, Ted and the boys had managed to saddle only two. Each had taken a wild ride. Each had been thrown. By the time we saw them again, they were at the pump, running water over their heads and looking defeated. Only Evan was pushing to try again.

"And him only fourteen!" Carl crowed as they all flopped down on the lawn with us girls. "Little old banty rooster! Pa, you should have seen 'im. He's gonna be one son-of-a-good bronc stomper."

"I was watching," said Mr. Scritsmier, who was dishing out ice cream. "No question about it. He stuck the longest."

Evan didn't look up. He just sat on the Scritsmiers' back steps spooning in that velvety ice cream and grinning.

No sooner had he emptied his bowl than Mary jumped up to fill it again. She didn't offer seconds to Ted, I noticed.

"You know what?" Evan said, once the twins quit fighting over the dasher. "I'd get on Murmur again if someone else would."

"Oh, my achin' back!" moaned Bones.

"Do it, do it!" cried Leon, the more murderous twin.

"Yeah, do it!" echoed Lena, banging her spoon on her bowl.

"Come on, then, younguns," said Carl. "It's mean-eyed Murmur or us." And he yanked his Texas-tooled boots back on his feet.

Bones flopped over and cut loose with his wolf howl. *"Woo-owooo!* It's the mustangs against the farm boys!"

In the end, the whole kit and caboodle of us trooped back to the corral to watch. All except Mrs. Scritsmier, who gathered up dishes, shaking her head. "There's homemade root beer," she said, "if any of you live through it."

After cheering for the horses—just to be ornery—Mary and Ruth and I, along with the sticky-faced twins, draped ourselves over the top rail of the corral to watch.

Ted and Carl singled out the one bronc that was halter broke—a dun-colored horse they were calling Murmur. She'd have made a fine parade horse with her creamy coat, black mane and haughty tail. But looks aren't everything. It took four pairs of hands to get a saddle on her again.

Once she was blindfolded and dancing nervously in the chute, the boys drew straws to see who'd go first. When we saw Ted's hat sail up in the air, we all cheered—Mary loudest of anyone.

We watched Ted climb to the top rail of their makeshift chute and grab the overhead bar. I held my breath as he swung a leg over and slowly lowered himself into the saddle.

Big mistake! Murmur apparently didn't like the feel of him at all and was instantly twisting and snorting, trying to buck. She mashed him into the boards with such fury, I thought for sure the chute was going to collapse.

I wiped my sweaty palms on my dress. How could he take such a pounding, such threshing around?

A shout went up. "Got your stirrups?"

"The gate, you ninnies!" came Ted's scared voice.

Coyote quick, Evan scrambled up the corral fence, but by then the Scritsmiers had wrenched it open themselves. Someone yanked off the horse's blindfold, and Murmur ripped out of the chute like a bullet.

"Ride 'em, cowboy!" shouted Mr. Scritsmier, slapping around with his hat, having the best time.

They bucked off across the corral away from us.

Talk about wild! That horse was hinged in the middle. First she'd fold up tight. Then down she'd come for a stiff-legged dive in the dirt. Same thing, over and over, hooves pounding fore and aft, fore and aft. I could feel the impact in my clammy palms—right through the railing.

Who'd named her Murmur, anyway? Try Bride of Satan!

When she got nowhere with bucking and plunging, she took up writhing and twisting. Still Ted managed to stick, though one loud *oomph* after another was forced out of him.

A couple of spins later, Murmur got up her meanness and headed straight for spectator row. We flew off that fence so fast! But I got a look at Ted's face. He wasn't about to let go of that saddle horn. Murmur might jar his teeth loose, but so far that wild-eyed dun had met her match in my wild-eyed brother.

And then it happened, and we were close enough to see it all. Ted lost his left stirrup. With the horse spinning and him slipping and all of us shouting "Hang on!"—well, we knew it, and I figured he knew it. His ride was about over.

Mary hid her face. Not me. I had to watch.

One more violent heave by Murmur and Ted went flying through the air.

Over the shouting and screaming, I heard a crack, then a thud as he hit the fence. Crumpling like a rag doll, he rolled facedown in the filth and dust of the corral.

The mustang, dirt spurting from her hooves, was still wound up like a spring and kept right on bucking.

Carl was after her in seconds, swatting with his hat and yelling for Bones to toss him a rope.

Ted wasn't moving. I started over the fence.

Ruth grabbed me from behind, but when I saw Mary top over and drop down inside, I pulled free and did the same.

"Out of there, girls!" yelled Mr. Scritsmier, who was running toward us. "You want to get killed?"

We ignored him. Murmur, by then, was at the far side of the corral, where Bones and Carl were struggling to restrain her. I wasn't afraid for myself.

Mary reached Ted first. I cried out on seeing so much blood—thick in his hair and starting to pool beneath him. I might have fainted except for Mary.

"Don't look!" she ordered. "Look away, you hear?"

In one swift move she lifted her skirt, unbuttoned her petticoat, yanked it off. Bunching it into a ball, she knelt and pressed it against the side of his head. For some crazy reason, I thought of Mama. What would she think about that unladylike behavior?

"Don't move him!" warned Mr. Scritsmier, pushing between us. "He'll come out of it. Head wounds are the bloodiest. Here now, Cassie, get back. Let him come to."

I gave Mr. Scritsmier a cross look and sat down on my heels. Ted was my brother; I wasn't going to get back. I stayed where I was.

I lifted the hand nearest me and squeezed the limp fingers. I was shocked, suddenly, by the strange weight of Ted's arm. I swung around to Mr. Scritsmier, who had his other wrist and was feeling for a pulse. "Is he dead?" I cried.

"See if he's breathing," came Evan's voice.

By then Ruth, who'd stayed at the fence, was sobbing loud enough for all of us. I wanted to hit her, to scream, "Stop that noise!"

"Let me at him," Mr. Scritsmier ordered, and this time he elbowed me away. He lifted Ted's eyelids. He felt his neck for a heartbeat.

"He's alive," he said finally. Satisfied, he checked the wound, then told Mary to keep the pressure on until they could get Ted's head in some clean wraps.

"I knew someone would get hurt fooling with those blame horses," he grumbled. "Carl! Bones!" He got to his feet. "Get over here!"

Then, to Mary and me, "He's gonna have a real goose egg for a souvenir."

A sob of relief exploded from my chest.

"Cassie?" Evan lifted me up and drew me away from the others. "Are you okay? You're white as a moonflower." He gave me a look I'll never forget. "He's not dead. Real bronc riders pull leather all the time." His grin, more than anything, made me feel better. "Getting knocked out—gosh, it's a badge, you know? He'll be a hero to the rest of us."

Blinking hard, I wiped my cheeks with the backs of my hands. I guess Evan knew how it felt to be so scared. Right then I wished I could hug him—or wished he'd hug me! But Mama wouldn't like it.

"Any ice left, Ma?" Bones yelled over our heads.

Mrs. Scritsmier was coming out of the house, drying her hands on an apron. She didn't yet know what had happened.

"Oh, my dears!" she cried when the twins ran up and told her. A minute later, Ruth and I were sent flying to the icehouse, the dugout where ice cut from the river was stored. We made baskets of our skirts to carry back the few shards we found in the straw. Not much.

Evan and Mr. Scritsmier moved Ted into the shade of a lilac bush, where he lay as limp as before. His color was better, at least. I could see his chest rising and falling. I stepped over the bottle of carbolic acid they were using to clean the wound, then watched as Mary and Mrs. Scritsmier wrapped Ted's head in strips of white sheeting.

With the ice folded securely in Mrs. Scritsmier's apron, Mary propped it against the side of Ted's bandaged head.

Mr. Scritsmier and the big boys went to hitch up, in case they'd have to go for the doctor. Or fetch Mama. Or take Ted home. One of the three. Nobody really knew what we should do.

Mostly we just waited with grave faces. I prayed, as well.

"He'll be dazed at first," Mrs. Scritsmier kept telling me, "but he'll come around. Fortunately, Cassie, the bleeding's stopped. We can be thankful he didn't break any bones."

"Ted, dear," Mary whispered as she cleaned up his face, "I'm so sorry. I shouldn't have egged you on!"

I tried to picture him sitting up, shaking out the cobwebs. Knowing Ted, he'd make light of it: "Okay, fellers, who greased that saddle?"

But he didn't come around. Long minutes passed and all I could think about, suddenly, was greeting the glorious new century without him. My throat tightened. What if he lived but stayed this way? What if he could never ride again? Or go spooning with his sweetheart? Or do any other wonderful, ordinary, everyday thing?

Ruth squeezed me around the waist. "The doctor will fix him up," she said in a whisper, as if reading my mind. "Maybe we should go play. You want to?"

"Ruth—no!" How could she think I'd want to play?

Now Evan was down on the ground opposite Mary, slapping Ted's other hand and arm as she was doing. When she asked for someone to take off Ted's boots ("For crying out loud!"), he took care of it. Mary had worked one year at the hospital in Hastings, so we did what she said.

Then Evan and I were both kneading Ted's feet and legs. The muscles were loose and floppy. *Like a dead chicken's,* I couldn't help thinking.

My heart hardened against Evan even as I worked there beside him. *This wouldn't have happened if he hadn't wanted a second go at that dang horse. Or if he were still in Montana. Where he belongs!*

I bit my lip until I could taste blood. Anger and fear were so mixed in me, I wanted to lash out as much as I wanted to cry.

By then Mr. Scritsmier and Carl had decided to take Ted home in the corn-picking wagon. It made sense. If he needed a doctor, our place was two miles closer to Blue Hill.

"Besides," Carl said, "a couple miles on that washboard of a road oughta bring him around."

The men took off the bangboard, then lifted him onto a blanket they'd thrown over a bed of straw. I crawled up beside him. Cradling his head, I was startled to find it so heavy—like a twenty-pound bag of feed. My foot, doubled under me, went to sleep in minutes.

But having a numb foot wasn't as bad as being eaten up. The straw was full of fleas. Real biters! We'd both end up covered with red welts.

The only comfort was that Ted couldn't feel a thing—not the bites, not the jolting, not the suffocating heat—as we bounced along in the bed of that tall-sided rig.

Behind us rode Evan, leading Prince and taking buckets of dust in his face. He sat tall in Papa's saddle, looking brown and healthy astride Millie. Pleased with himself, even.

I looked down at Ted, who was gray as a mushroom, and set my jaw.

Evan the Infidel! Evan the Infidel!

The phrase turned over and over in my mind, as relentlessly as the wagon wheels bearing us along. We were the ones who'd taken an unbeliever to the bosom of our family. What could we expect? We'd brought the trouble on ourselves.

Chapter 12

Days passed, a good part of a week, and Ted lay right where they'd put him—on my bed in the parlor. Unmoving.

Papa had gone for the doctor first thing Monday morning. Both men, it turned out, had been up all night—Papa with praying over Ted, the doctor trying to pull a woman through inflammation of the bowels.

All the doctor could tell us, after lifting Ted's eyelids and getting a glassy stare in return, was that Ted was in a coma, due to concussion. "He's had a very wicked blow."

We already know that, I thought, glaring at the doctor skeptically. I stood by as he felt for broken bones, my arms over my chest, upset that he wasn't asking me about the accident.

In the end, he gave Mama a long list of instructions about taking care of Ted in case the coma went on. "The swelling's not good," he added, "but we won't know till later if he's had brain damage."

Then he and Papa sat down for coffee and Mama clumped around fixing them a platter of fried bread. The doctor lit his pipe and smoked. They talked about the hog cholera epidemic and the trainload of hogs bound for Chicago. They talked about the hay languishing in the fields and the corn crop burning up.

"When was that last big rain?" Papa asked, as if weather were the most important thing on his mind. "July twenty-six?"

How could Papa sit there and be so calm? And poor Mama! She was crazy with worry, you could see it in her face. How could those men just sit there talking weather and crops?

The doctor did pat Mama's hand when he finally left. "Let me know if you can't handle this, Rachel. You may need a trained nurse before it's over."

Before it's over! What did he mean by that?

After the doctor left, Mama sent John and me straightaway to the gypsy camp on the river. Thank goodness for Queenie, who dropped everything and came back to the house with us. Her hair might have been graying, but in her bright tent-size dress and yellow scarf, her glass beads swinging, she was the only rainbow in that gloomy place.

The next few days we walked around scared, although we never talked about how scared. We went through the motions of living, always with an eye toward Ted's still form in the middle of the parlor. I was no longer fussing about my bed or Evan or any other paltry thing that had bothered me earlier. All I wanted was for Ted to open his eyes and talk to us, to be the big lug of a brother he'd always been.

Each day the house heated up to over a hundred. We spent hours wringing out towels in a basin we'd set on the library table, then draping them over Ted. We had to keep him moist, Queenie told Mama. So once an hour or more, one of us was squeezing liquid into his mouth from little sops we'd fashioned.

The doctor had said he might be able to swallow. "Reflexively" was how he'd put it, adding, "if the coma isn't too deep."

For the first thirty hours, the water we squeezed into his mouth either choked him or rolled back out. By the time his Adam's apple finally moved and we could see he was swallowing, it was midmorning Tuesday. He swallowed four more times before Mama collapsed on her knees, sobbing, "Thank God, thank God!"

When she couldn't stop crying, Queenie and I lifted her up and put her to bed. She hadn't slept since her nap on Sunday.

I'd rarely heard our parents at odds, but they were that week. In strong words, Papa blamed Mama for letting Ted go off to break horses on the

Sabbath, insisting he was paying for it now. Mama, tight-lipped, simply quit talking to him and went on doing what she had to. I felt sorry for them both, but mostly for Ted.

The only fun we had that week was when Queenie hung the wash so fast she forgot to look behind her. Suddenly, from outside, we heard a howl that stiffened the hairs on my arms. I ran to the back window. John's pet crow had started at the far end of the clothesline and was plucking clothespins off as fast as Queenie was putting them on. All her nice white wash was on the ground!

John ran screaming out of the house, afraid she'd kill his beloved. If anything could have wakened Ted, their shouting match over Cawky would have done it.

With Papa and Evan haying from dawn to dusk, and with Mama's hands so misshapen, it was big, capable Queenie who kept us going. Ted was a dead weight, but he had to be turned. The wound needed cleaning and his limbs needed exercising— to say nothing of personal care, for which Mama sent me out of the room. The cooking and cleaning fell to me, but we'd have been hard-pressed to manage without Queenie.

As word spread about Ted, the entire countryside came calling. Folks brought pies, cakes, hams, peaches, crusty loaves of bread and every variety of pickle known to man.

Most of our visitors also had suggestions for how to revive Ted. Some were so strange, Mama and

Queenie were moved to ridicule after they left. What good would it do, for instance, to plaster Ted with a poultice soaked in skunk lard?

A laughing spell Mama couldn't contain was when deaf and toothless Mrs. Knightly suggested she "git ahold" of a pint of stout. She was to warm it up a smidge. "But only a smidge, dearie."

With Queenie and Mama both listening, she made the most of her moment, taking her own sweet time blowing across the coffee she'd saucered.

"Next, find a nice, quiet place to sit"—there was another pause before she pushed her face right into Mama's—*"then drink it yerself!"*

Mama burst out laughing.

"Aye, it's an old Irish remedy." Mrs. Knightly sat back, looking satisfied. "One I've used many a time!"

A bonus for us all was getting to see Mary Cunningham twice during the week. The Scritsmiers loaned her to us—sent her over on horseback to spend the day. She helped with morning milking, baked bread Mama had started the night before, polished the stove, scrubbed floors, then filled the air with the clean smell of starching. All before noon.

In the afternoons, while Mama rested from being up at night, Mary fussed over Ted, straightening his hair and patting his face with ointments to keep him cool. That was my favorite time.

"See how the witch hazel brings out his freckles?" she'd say when we were alone. And we'd smile. We both loved him a lot.

She sang to Ted as well. Trail songs and old-timey songs of the South. The rest of us would listen. Even John.

Mary was convinced he could hear her, even if he was in a coma. She said we should talk to him. Read to him.

"He's not somewhere else, Cassie, as you might think. He's right here. We have to give him some of our strength."

I didn't tell anyone how gently she kissed his eyes when no one was in the room but us.

Thursday morning, an evangelist who'd known Papa years before at Shenandoah College in Iowa came clopping up our lane just as Papa and Evan were coming in from the hayfield at noon.

Reverend and Mrs. Peabody stayed for hours and just about prayed us to death. Even though Papa had a crop to get in, the two men knelt at Ted's bedside, imploring God until I thought Ted might just rise up and shout, "Enough! I'm well already!"

The worst of it was the healing prayer.

The reverend had all of us circle the bed, placing our hands up and down the length of Ted's body. It must have been 105 degrees in that room, but we were each, in turn, to say a prayer for Ted's recovery.

"I can feel the power of faith in this circle," the reverend said, his eyes closed, his head tilted heavenward. "God will not deny us if we truly believe. Beginning with you, Mrs. Peabody, let us pray for divine intervention."

John came next, promising he'd be good every day, that he'd not sneak raisins or tell lies or beg, if only God would make Ted well.

I whispered a prayer next, shorter than John's.

When it was Evan's turn, we waited. And I worried. How could he pray if he didn't believe? He'd told me he was "nothing." Hadn't he told Papa? A trickle of sweat rolled all the way down my back. When the room started to whirl and the smell of carbolic acid and the reverend's stale breath threatened to overcome me, I opened my eyes.

"Your turn." John was urging Evan in whispers.

Evan shook his head.

A choking sound came from Papa's end. His eyes were open, too. And blazing. "You—will—pray!" he said in a voice so angry it scared me.

But Evan's lips were stitched together. He shook his head again. I stared down at Reverend Peabody's clean white shoes and knew Evan wasn't going to pray, no matter what.

"Get away!" Papa shouted suddenly, and in two strides he smacked Evan's hands up and away from Ted. "Out of here! Your spirit's unholy!"

"Ike!" Mama cried. "Mind what you're doing!"

By then the reverend, too, was saying, "Go, go!"

Evan fled.

John followed before anyone could stop him.

Queenie made a whole sentence of *tsk tsk* sounds, and Mama looked ready to cry.

When no one made a move to go after John, the healing prayers went on, rising to Reverend

Peabody's fiery crescendo and Papa's earnest final "Amen!"

Papa's unshaven face was dark with fatigue and worry. No wonder! He and Evan had been doing the work of four men.

Afterward I sat for a minute in John's swing behind the house, wishing those people had never come. And Evan! Couldn't he have said a simple little prayer, just "Please, God, heal Ted" or something? Papa, whom I'd never seen act so mean, had shoved him right out of the circle. It was like making him an orphan all over again.

I found John and Evan on a bench at the side of the barn, talking in whispers as if they were still in some holy presence.

"Evan doesn't know how to pray," John said, trying to sound sad in the face of things. "That's how come he didn't."

"I can speak for myself," Evan snapped. "I *don't* pray is what I told you."

"Maybe for Ted you might have—" I didn't finish. I felt sorrier for him than I wanted to let on. "Anyway, Papa will get over it, huh, John? He's always sorry afterwards."

"This is different," Evan mumbled. *"I'm* different. Pa and Ma and us—we never were churchy." He sat with his elbows on his knees, playing with a piece of straw and not looking at either of us. "I'm not like you people. I can't abide false pretensions, so I shouldn't even be here."

"I think"—John suddenly lit up—"we should do

exactly what Evan says. Papa would forgive him then."

Wearily I dropped down on the old scarred bench beside John. "And what's that?"

"He says we should give Ted some brandy. Not enough to make him—you know—tipsy."

I spun around to confront Evan. "What a thing to tell him!"

I watched as his face reddened. He didn't yet realize John repeated every single thing he heard.

"It worked for us, that's all," he said with a shrug.

"What do you mean?"

He finished bending the straw into stairsteps, then tossed it. "My little brother Tilden. When he had typhoid. He'd turned blue up to the elbows and knees. Doctor said he'd be gone by morning."

I stared hard at Evan. He wouldn't be making this up.

"A woman from up on the mountain said she'd had a vision she was needed. She came down an' talked Ma into giving him brandy." He showed me how much between his thumb and forefinger. "By morning his fever broke. He lived another two years."

I didn't mention it, but several good church members had already suggested brandy. I'd put it in the same category as skunk lard.

Papa, of course, wouldn't have a drop of liquor in the house.

I stood up to go back inside. I couldn't linger. Mama would need me.

Evan got up, too, saying, "Tell your pa I'll go throw on another load. The wind's up. We're in for some weather, if you ask me."

"Don't let those Peoplebodys eat up our chocolate cake!" John called after me as I walked away.

Lena Myers's buttermilk fudge cake stood on a cut-glass stand on the sideboard. In plain sight. It didn't stand a chance.

Crossing to the house, I realized Evan was right—the wind was up. The first breeze in days. I also noticed a thick, greenish curtain hanging in the west. Good! We needed a rattling thunderstorm to cool things off.

But only half of Papa's hay was in stacks. Maybe if I told the Peabodys a cyclone was coming, they'd jump in their fancy buggy and hightail it back to Hastings.

Too late. I could smell fresh coffee as soon as I hit the porch steps. Our visitors—plump as quail—were already seated at the table. Since Queenie had gone back to the river to do for her own, serving a meal would be up to Mama and me.

I didn't go straight inside. I turned into the breeze first and flapped my skirt up and down to cool me off underneath.

"Cassie, whatever are you doing out there?" came Mama's voice.

Poor Mama, cross and worn out.

I suddenly found myself turning against my own papa, who was trying so hard to please company that he couldn't think of Mama. Or of his blood nephew's feelings. Or of Ted, either, it seemed, lying there so still, needing to be turned and tended to.

Papa's laughter drifted out. Mr. Peabody was telling a story our papa was finding very funny. It wasn't right!

I stomped on inside. So let Papa's hay rot in the field! A gully-washer would serve him right.

I was getting more like my mama every day.

Chapter 13

As soon as the "People-bodys" left, Papa went straight back to the hayfield. Evan, and now Bones, who'd come over to help, were already out with the team and their pitchforks, hurrying to beat the rain.

Queenie came back over so that Mama could get some sleep. Then, hot as it was, she made up the fire and set two flatirons on the stove. The clean clothes—dampened and rolled—had been stored in our copper boiler for two days.

"Too much company, huh?" she remarked as I finished drying the dishes. "I'll iron till the weather sends me scuttlin' out of here." She popped a wet finger against the hot iron. "Looks like you'll get stuck with supper and the milkin' both, young lady."

I could think of three or four other things I'd get stuck with, too, but there was no use whining.

It was time for Ted to have some nourishment, so I made a thin mix of applesauce and honey and tried spooning it in with John's baby spoon. John wanted to help, so he stood on a stool and wiped up whatever escaped.

"Is this how you used to feed me?" he asked innocently. The look on his face made me smile. Good thing, because I felt more like crying. Ted had grown so thin and pale, his cheeks were caving in.

After we finished, I washed his face with cool water and helped Queenie get him into a freshly ironed shirt. Then John and I sat on the floor, leaning against the bed, and I read aloud the chapter from *Little Women* in which Beth comes down with scarlet fever. It was very sad. Now and then, John would sneak up a hand and pat whatever part of Ted he could reach.

Pretty soon I noticed that Queenie was acting peculiar. Twice she stuck in her head and told John to go play outside while he had a chance. But we were at an exciting place, and he was listening open-mouthed.

Before long she was back shutting all the windows. The parlor, closed up, would be hotter than the kitchen. I wished she'd tend to her things and let us tend to ours!

About then we started hearing little clicking

sounds at the windowpanes. I stopped reading to listen.

"Is it hail?" John asked.

"Uh-uh. Don't think so. Just stuff blowing around."

The next time Queenie came lumbering in, she reached all the way across Ted and tapped me smartly on top of the head. She was waving a slender brown bottle in the air and pointing vigorously down at John. When she hooked a thumb at the door, I finally caught on. She wanted him out of there.

I snapped the book shut. "Queenie's right," I said. "Go find Sticky and have a gallop before we get shut in. I'll read to you and Ted again tonight."

"Think he likes *Little Women*?" John asked as he got up off the floor. I nodded back. "I do!" he said. For once he didn't argue but skipped out, calling, "Sticky, where are you?"

Queenie bustled around to my side of the bed as soon as we heard the screen door slam.

"Five days is too long." Her whispering was urgent. "He's going flabby on us. Your mama and papa . . . they'd never in the world turn to the medicinals, but likker has its uses."

She walked to the east window to make sure John was gone, then came back, uncapping the bottle. She passed it under my nose. "It's brandy, that's all. Won't hurt him, but it might shock his system enough to bring 'im around."

My heart started to pound. What did she want, for us to go against Papa and Mama?

"I have to get back to the river, Cassie. Storm's rollin' in fast. Clothes—oh my! We've got clothes hangin' out all over.

"Now listen to me. Make yourself a nice clean sop. There's less than a quarter cup in here. Drop it in his mouth a little at a time. Easy like. You're better at this than any of us."

I opened my mouth to object.

"Don't worry. Your mama's gonna stay asleep awhile."

"But Queenie, can't you? Papa would kill me!"

"I'm not family, you are. When you're finished, toss that bottle behind the privy. No one'll ever see it. You get caught," she said with a wink, "tell 'em it's applejack. Same thing, but it sounds better."

I took the bottle in my hands as if it were poison.

"Cassie Tucker!" She pulled me up by the shoulders. "You've borne a woman's load for some time now. You can do this!" We were nose to nose before she let me down. "I can't see that lovely young man dying because we're too busy prayin' and carryin' on. Trying what's right at hand takes faith, too."

It was only four o'clock, but the house grew frighteningly dark after Queenie left. I stood there taking quick breaths, thinking about what she'd said and listening for sounds from Mama's room. There was only the gusting wind and that funny *tick-tick-ticking* against the panes.

I didn't know what to do. I did know that John would burst in if it got too bad outside, and then I wouldn't be able to do anything.

I thought of Evan's little brother. Maybe they

were right, Queenie and Evan and some of the others. Queenie, of all people, wouldn't do anything to hurt Ted. He was her favorite.

I twisted a square of cloth to make a sop, then poured the brandy into a bowl. Gingerly, I dipped the sop and sniffed at it. The sharp sting in my nose brought me up short.

Maybe I should taste it first.

I wet a finger with brandy and stuck it in my mouth. *Yecch!* I snatched up a corner of Ted's sheet and scrubbed at my tongue. How could people drink such nasty stuff?

But they do. And it doesn't kill them. At least I'd never heard of death due to brandy.

My hands shook as I opened Ted's mouth and squeezed a few drops onto his tongue. His lips pursed. He didn't like it, either, but it went down.

I gave him more on the next try, then jumped a foot when he choked. Terrified, I dropped the sop and lifted his head. He went on making a sour face, but once again I could tell he was swallowing.

I elevated his head with an extra pillow, thinking that might help, then picked up the sop and started in again. The ticking of the clock was like cannon in my ears, but, a little at a time, Ted was, indeed, taking the brandy.

"I'm sorry," I whispered once. "It's bad-tasting medicine, isn't it? Horrible! But it's going to make you well." I hoped I'd be forgiven if it was all a lie.

Suddenly I was no longer afraid for myself. I was scared only that we might lose Ted. If Queenie thought he was dying—Queenie, who was almost a family member, who often knew things other people didn't—if *she* was scared, well, so was I.

With patience I never dreamed I had, I administered drop after drop of the brandy. Most of what went in also went down.

Very gradually Ted's cheeks were turning pink. How could it be hurting him? He looked better than he had for days, even if he did smell like a saloon.

It took a while to finish what was in the bottle. Finally, after feeling Ted's heartbeat, making sure he was breathing, I ran outside to the privy, pretending urgency in case John saw me.

The air by then was full of dust. It swirled up from the ground and blasted me in the face. The sky, what I could see of it, was dull as pewter.

I tossed the bottle into the weeds behind the outhouse, spent two minutes inside, then came out leaning against wind that blew my skirt over my head. I usually liked being out in storms, but recalling how Mrs. Kagley had been knocked flat in July, I made a beeline for the house.

What a weird storm! No thunder or lightning yet, but the sun was blotted out as thoroughly as if we were having an eclipse.

Gripping the screen door to keep it from swinging back, I could barely make out John shooing chickens into the henhouse. I'd check Ted first, then come back out and give him a hand.

I was no sooner in off the porch than I heard Ted calling me. I thought I was imagining things at first, but then my heart did a somersault and I knew.

I ran into the parlor. He was trying to raise himself up.

"Cassie?" His eyes were wide open, yet to speak seemed a terrible struggle. "Get the cows in! Big storm's coming!"

"*Mama!*" I screamed at the top of my lungs.

I needn't have. She'd heard him, too.

The next instant we had our arms around his neck, hugging and kissing him and crying, all at once.

He kept saying, "Storm's coming," although I'll never know, for the life of me, how he knew.

"Never mind the cows," Mama said with a laugh. "For now, the milk's better off where it is!"

We all held each other some more and the two of us mopped our faces. I'm sure Ted didn't know what to make of such a display. He must have wondered why he was lying in the parlor, head wrapped, being fussed over by the likes of us.

The smell of brandy was everywhere, I realized shortly. I crossed my fingers behind me, hoping against hope. Too late. Mama had already spotted the evidence.

"I gave him brandy. Queenie said to." I blinked back a flood of angry tears. "Mama, I didn't want him to die!"

"Oh, my little girl!" She pulled me close, crying all over again, but into my hair this time.

"Cassie, we mustn't tell!" She held me away suddenly, her eyes boring into mine. "Do you understand what I'm saying? There are some secrets a woman needs to keep."

I nodded, knowing exactly what she meant.

She didn't realize it, I'm sure, but she'd just called me a woman. Right then I felt like one, too.

"Get rid of this first," she said, lifting the brown-stained cloth by the fingertips. "Bury it! Then go find John. You two can run to the hayfield and tell Papa.

"Thanks be to God!" Mama shouted, with not a trace of weariness about her. "Our prayers have been answered! Ted's back and rain's on the way!"

Chapter 14

Mama was wrong about one thing. It didn't rain. There was no downpour, only the worst dust storm you can imagine.

We didn't go to the hayfield, either. We couldn't have found it. Once Mama realized what was happening, she tied a scarf over my face and sent me out after John.

Ducking into the wind, I ran toward a sound I knew well—the banging of the chicken coop door. My eyes were smarting before I'd gone ten feet, and my skirt ballooned around me. I tried turning my back to the wind, but that didn't help, either.

John saw me coming and started screaming, "I can't shut it!" His face was dirty and tear-streaked,

97

but he wasn't about to leave his chickens until we'd dragged shut that heavy door. No easy job, even for two. To make matters worse, Cawky clung to the roof, squawking at us the whole time, his feathers ruffled comically.

John finally found the stick we used at night, and I forced it into the hasp to lock the door.

We grabbed hands then and ran back to the house. I didn't tell him about Ted. I wanted him to discover for himself.

John stood a long time at the parlor doorway, shyly staring in. He was wondering, I suppose, why his big brother didn't jump right up and be like he was before.

When Ted asked whose little boy that was, John threw me an anguished look and slipped out of the room.

A bit later he wanted to know where Ted had been all that time. "Is he back for good?" I detected a slight quiver when he pulled me down to whisper, "How come he forgot me?"

We spent the tail end of that afternoon bunching rugs under doors, covering dishes, putting food-stuffs in the chest. After Mama showed me how, I went through the house—upstairs and down—with a table knife, stuffing rags around the window frames.

It was all for naught. Dust finer than powdered sugar drifted along the sills and sifted into the cupboards. Worse yet, it filled our mouths with grit.

In the midst of so much commotion, Ted thrilled us by sitting up, with Mama's help, and drinking a full glass of buttermilk. Mostly he seemed content to lie there, watching with big eyes as the rest of us bustled around.

Wind and sand continued battering us, howling around the house and peppering the windows. Real dark was coming on fast. I peered out a window. Where were they? Why didn't they quit and come home?

"Get out the lamps," Mama told me, starting to sound anxious herself. "They'll never find us in this."

John followed me into the kitchen. "But it's not night yet, Cassie." He was persisting again. "Is it the end of the world?"

I gave him what I hoped was a withering look. He'd heard too much end-of-the-world stuff from the twins.

"Well, *is* it?" he demanded.

"Of course not! It's so Papa and them can see the house."

I set lamps in each of the east windows and hung the lantern out on the porch, its bail over a hook. Mama, in the meantime, filled an iron pot with water and stoked the fire. The cornmeal she stirred in was standard invalid fare at our house, but it would also be tonight's supper. For once I didn't mind. My heart was so full of joy over Ted, I'd lick dust off the floor and pronounce it delicious.

Bones was forced to sleep over that night. The men, we soon discovered, had had a scary struggle lashing the load to the rack and then finding their way back. Unharnessing and feeding kept them in the barn a maddeningly long time. Mama wanted to rush right out and tell them about Ted. I was the one who wouldn't let her.

"You can't, Mama! You don't know! It'll blow you over."

I thought sure they'd break down when they walked in and saw Ted. He was propped up with pillows. The bandage was gone. He was wearing a fresh shirt and his hair was combed. (Sort of. I'd done it.) He looked as pink and rested as the Blue Hill banker.

"H'lo, Papa," he said weakly.

I guess it isn't a man's way to break into tears. Not like with Mama and me. Instead, the parlor erupted with enough noise to lift our old house right off its foundation.

"Oh, my lord!" cried Bones, who danced around slapping his legs, calling Ted a "sod-hoppin' bronc buster" and a few other things that weren't so polite.

Mama and Papa themselves couldn't leave off praising God. And John couldn't quit laughing at the "masks" the men wore in from the fields: the white eyeholes popping out of dirty faces.

I left the room to go dish up the mush, hoping the subject of brandy would never come up in my presence.

At the table that night, joining hands, Papa asked God to forgive his "inclement outburst" during the afternoon when the Peabodys were there. "Lord, I'd rather you cut out my tongue," he prayed, "than allow me to say such words to anyone again."

Mama served Papa first after the prayer and patted his shoulder. John gave me a sly poke. I sighed with relief. Bones, looking rather mystified, simply plunged into his supper—hot mush with butter, new turnips from the garden, bread and butter and, of course, grit. No one complained. I'd have smacked them if they had.

We trooped into the parlor afterward, where Mama was still spooning mush into Ted's mouth.

"You work like you did today, Evan," Papa said so everyone could hear, "and you'll be a top hay hand. Pitchin' and loadin' both."

Evan's ears turned red. When Papa squeezed the back of his neck, then playfully shook his head around, Evan couldn't hold back a big old Tucker smile. For a minute there, he looked exactly like Papa.

They'd worked side by side to keep a crop from blowing away. The storm—or maybe it was Ted—had wrought the miracle that brought them together again.

I tried to remember how things were before Evan, when we were a family of five instead of six, and was surprised at how much I liked having him with us.

Chapter 15

It was the end of September before Ted was up and able to help with the farm. No one, not even the doctor, thought it would take so long. Not only was he slow getting back strength, he was slow relearning the simplest things. It was as if he'd never known how to walk, climb stairs, dress himself, even comb his hair. John had a hilarious time teaching him how to clap hands.

Ted had no memory of being bucked off a horse and never spoke of it, even when Carl and Bones supplied him with details. In the end, Papa said we probably shouldn't bring it up.

In the meantime, my big lug of a brother ate us out of house and home.

How I wished the neighbors would come back bearing gifts of delicious food! Nobody did. Only Mary, who rode over every Sunday afternoon, always bringing a basket of goodies she'd baked. She would read Ted interesting tidbits from the almanac, then listen as he falteringly read back to her.

Because of Ted's slow recovery, we had to give up going to the street fair in Hastings. I'd been dreaming about it all year, but Mama insisted it wouldn't be right to go and leave Ted behind.

"Not another word, Cassie!" she snapped the day I crossed the line between persistence and out-and-out begging. "We can't afford the train ride, let alone treats."

That, I knew, was the real reason. Why couldn't grown-ups say in plain words what they really meant?

Without rain, everyone's grain had come in less than full. Our corn crop, too, was puny, which meant we'd have to sell off some hogs. I knew all that. Didn't they think I'd understand?

Even Papa had to give up something important. He'd been hoping to go to Clay Center to hear William Jennings Bryan, having missed him earlier in Red Cloud. The Silver-Tongued Orator, as he was called, was the farmer's friend and about the only politician Papa trusted. But it would mean buying a train ticket, and Mama insisted we three have shoes for school. She blamed her own foot problems on having to wear two left shoes, castoffs, for much too long during her childhood as they waited for crops to ripen.

Thinking to console me, Papa brought home a copy of *The Adams County Democrat* so that I could read about the fair. It didn't help. To know there were a hundred flower-decorated carriages, a milelong midway, parades, bands, ascension balloons . . . Well! Reading about it left me limp with longing.

I *was* consoled, however, by the present Ruth bought me at the fair: a splendid diary for the first year of the twentieth century. It was wrapped in white tissue paper and tied with a plaid ribbon I could use for school. The year *1900* was imprinted on the cover in gold. I couldn't thank her enough.

Despite disappointments, things had nearly returned to normal by the time October rolled around. Mornings walking to school were more fun with John along. And although I missed Miss Deffenbach, who was now John's teacher, Mr. Osgood was tolerable.

"Fall," I gushed the first morning we wore sweaters, "is my favorite time of year."

"Along with spring, summer and winter," John had added, looking wise.

I laughed. Among the Tuckers, being impartial about Nebraska's seasons was as important, in its way, as being impartial about family.

"Want to know how I picture the seasons?" I asked John. "I see a giant Ferris wheel. Winter's the chair at the bottom. As it goes up, it becomes spring. Over the top an' it's summer. Autumn's last. It's that falling-down season I like best."

"Me too," John said companionably, one arm going like a wheel.

The second Saturday of October, Evan and I piled into the wagon before dawn. We were heading for Blue Hill. I hadn't been for ages. With Ted riding again, he and Mary had planned a ramble and were taking John along. That mean there'd be room in the wagon for all the creamery stuff, a load of potatoes, and us!

The air had a shivery feel to it as we left the yard. Noisily I filled my lungs with the morning's smoky smells, and I buttoned my jacket to my chin.

As daylight came on, we could see how pale the cottonwoods had grown. Half their leaves were gone. Same with the ash and box elders. Cold nights had been at work thinning them out.

The musty leaves crunched pleasantly under the horses' hooves and the wheels. Papa's "Giddyup, boys!" and the slap of reins were the only sounds breaking the stillness.

I think Evan was as excited to be going to town as I was. We rode the whole way swinging our legs off the back.

It wasn't until we spotted the tall grain elevator looming at our end of town that Evan confessed to a bad case of nervousness. Not because he'd never been to Blue Hill, he said, but because Mr. Mc-Cleery at the Mercantile was going to measure him for the Sunday suit he'd promised. He'd never been fitted before.

I grinned. Evan scared of something? He'd come a thousand miles alone, dispatched rattlesnakes, stuck to a devil horse, and just yesterday had outrun the neighbor's meanest bull. He'd even stood up to Papa, hadn't he? And got away with it.

"Don't know if I can stand still that long." His nose wrinkled with distaste. "You know, like your ma says I have to."

"It won't hurt too much," I said, wickedly dragging out the *too*. "Queenie's stuck me plenty. You'll have a few spots of blood. A dab of pennyroyal will take care of 'em."

"Pins!" he snorted. "I forgot about pins!" He unhooked the rear chain, jumped from the wagon and took off running. I wasn't fooled. He loved showing off. In minutes he was jumping back on.

The rest of the way we talked about school and what he could expect, having enrolled late because Papa needed him. Although he listened to me jabber, he asked so many questions I figured he was as nervous about school as he was about the fitting.

I did discover he'd been tested and passed on *McGuffey's Sixth Eclectic Reader* the year before.

"Where will that put me here?" he wanted to know.

"Ahead of me," I said with a dismal face. I was still reading from *McGuffey's Fifth* and might be until I died. Too bad. I loved novels far more than schoolbooks. Strict Mr. Osgood wouldn't allow any "pleasure reading," as he called it, until I got better at long division.

"Last year," I told Evan, "Miss Deffenbach let me read whatever I pleased." (She also let us watch Mrs. Lindsey, whom we called Linsey-woolsey, dance on the roof of her nearby dugout, as she did on occasion.)

We were passing the livery stable when Mama called me forward in the wagon. She counted out twenty cents for muslin I was to buy, then pushed an extra nickel into my palm. "Spend it on whatever takes your eye. We'll find you when we're finished shopping for Evan." Seeing me frown, she added, "Don't worry! You can't get lost in Blue Hill."

I wasn't worried about that. I was disappointed. I'd wanted to watch Evan being fitted for his church suit, an item that would set Mr. McCleery back a whopping $2.75, at the least.

"Listen, Cassie," Mama went on, "if you wear yourself out, come back to Ma Sommerfeld's. She'll let you wait in the parlor."

We were stopping there next to make a delivery, so Mama went in and arranged things. I got out, too, and watched as Papa and Evan wrestled a heavy cream can into the boardinghouse kitchen. Eggs packed in straw went in next, along with a basket of red potatoes.

While everyone was busy, I peeked in through the oval glass of Ma Sommerfeld's front door. I liked what I saw: shiny end tables, red velvet settees, glass prisms on a gas chandelier. There were gleaming spittoons by every chair! And in the corner, a piano. I'd make sure I got tired early.

After an hour exploring the dusty main street and watching the trains, and another hour sampling likely-looking shops along the boardwalk, I surely was tired. But by then I was at the other end of town from the boardinghouse and my stomach was growling.

Then I saw a sign in the window of Nelson's Hardware—a sign they'd just put up—and it stopped me in my tracks.

BIG SALE TODAY
HOME COMFORT RANGES
FREE BISCUITS AND COFFEE

I shaded my eyes and peered in. Ladies were sitting at one of the small tables, sipping coffee and enjoying free biscuits. Farther back, it seemed a salesman was demonstrating the superior qualities of a shiny, nickel-trimmed cookstove.

I stood outside, fidgeting with my purchases as a dray and single horse went past, then mules pulling a wagonload of corn. People called to each other in the busy street, and a boy John's age chased a cat, yelling "Come 'ere, stupid cat!"

I tugged at the fingers of my gloves. I really wanted some of that coffee, whose aroma was about to overcome me. I was rarely allowed such a treat at home.

I stole another look through the plate glass window.

I could say I was shopping for my mother, couldn't I? After all, she could use a new stove. Our oversized cob-eater was ancient, nothing like the sleek new range in Nelson's.

Moments later I was inside, seating myself at the last empty table in the small space that had been cleared. I smiled and an older lady smiled back. Everyone seemed friendly, even the salesman with the pointy mustache, who seemed to be demonstrating to one or two people at a time. He spoke so crisply, I figured he hadn't come from around there.

"My mother's meeting me," I told the lady who came to the table with butter and jam. Now, *she,* more likely, was from Blue Hill. Her apron was the same pattern as Mama's. It had been a flour sack first.

When the plate of steaming biscuits came, I dug in. Never had anything tasted so good! Then, promptly, a cup of coffee arrived. I stirred in cream and a teaspoon of sugar and let my mind float off into realms of ecstasy. How fine to be waited on!

It wasn't Mama who found me there. I had just smiled my thanks for a coffee-warming when Evan walked in through the door. He looked a foot taller in his new boots.

"Cassie," he hissed as he slid into the chair beside me. "What are you doing here? This isn't for just . . . *anybody*!"

"It isn't? But I saved some for you." I indicated the fluffy biscuits and jar of jam. "Ask her." I pointed. "She'll bring you some coffee. It's free."

Evan's face rivaled the color of the jam, but he stayed. I slathered a biscuit with butter and jam and made him take it. He finally did, but hunched over it as if to hide the fact.

He flatly refused to ask for coffee.

Presently he showed me the new saddlebag Papa insisted he have for school, since he'd be riding Millie back and forth. I sniffed at the new leather and poked a hand into the pockets, where I found, of all things, a letter addressed to him.

"Can you believe it sat at the post office a whole week? Look. See where it's from?" He let me read the Montana postmark.

Naturally I hoped he'd tell me who wrote it or what it said, but he put it right back into the saddlebag. For once I had manners enough not to ask.

Mrs. Scritsmier, wearing a big feathered hat, came sweeping through the door next. She looked aghast to see Evan and me sitting there big as you please, but Ruth, who trailed in behind her, was full of smiles.

"Cassie, what a surprise!" Ruth said. Then, "H'lo, Evan."

While her mother went back into the store to buy lamp mantles, the three of us made polite talk. Then, remembering, I presented Ruth with one of the two identical hair combs I'd bought with my nickel.

"So we'll be twins," I said as she exclaimed over it. "Wear it Monday, okay? It'll be Evan's first day. I guess we'd better try to look—um—pretty, huh?"

I giggled saying such a thing. I then passed around the still-warm biscuits and insisted we finish them off before Ruth's mother came back. Evan, too, was persuaded to have one more.

That's why we were caught unawares when the

spiffy salesman sidled over and tapped Evan on the shoulder.

"Tell me," he said with exaggerated politeness, "which one of these lovely ladies is your wife—and which the daughter?"

Wife! Daughter!

Evan choked down the biscuit and grabbed up his saddlebag, a horrified look on his face. He was ready to bolt.

"Oh, never mind!" The man patted Evan back down. "I'll get to you folks next." I couldn't take my eyes off the waxed tips of his twitching mustache as he said, "You've certainly been patient."

As soon as his back was turned, I whispered "Bye!" to Ruth. Evan and I grabbed our things and tumbled out of there. Around the corner, the two of us laughed until tears ran down our cheeks.

"Cassie, you ninny!" he kept saying. "What'd I tell you?"

We didn't make it home that Saturday before the sky opened up and dumped on us. Evan and I had nothing to put over our heads but an already wet blanket Papa had used to keep the cream cans cool. Mama, who was always prepared, had her umbrella up at the first drop. It couldn't have helped much against the deluge hitting us sideways.

Up on the wagon seat, Papa was snapping the reins and hollering at Doug and Barney, all but cussing. "Giddyup, you lazy rascals!"

Evan and I huddled together under the smelly blanket, bouncing along on the lumpy bundles that contained his store-bought clothes. The new saddle-bag was wedged between us.

We were still a half mile from home—mud flying everywhere—when he shouted his news at my ear.

"Miss Hallie . . . she still wants to be my guardian, to make sure I get schooling." He pointed to the saddlebag. "She's been to see a lawyer." His eyes gleamed at me out of the dark.

"You wouldn't go live with her, would you?"

"Don't know," he shouted back. "She's going to Omaha at Christmas. Wants to get off the train here to see if I'm all right."

I looked away. He wouldn't leave us now, would he? Now that Papa had bought him a saddlebag and outfitted him in such fine new clothes?

You can't go! I wanted to shout. It would be—I groped for a word and came up with Mama's—it would be *unseemly!*

I pulled my head out from under the blanket and let the cold rain smack me in the face. Didn't he like being with us? Was it all Papa's doing, making him pray and go to church when he didn't believe, working him to death like any old hired hand?

I didn't have other cousins in Nebraska; he had to stay. We all liked him, couldn't he see that? Especially John. Oh my! John, still so tender, would die if Evan went away.

Tears and rain mixed and ran down my cheeks. I wished I could tell him what was in my heart: *You can't leave us . . . now that we've started to love you!*

Chapter 16

I jumped off the wagon at the gate. Forgetting myself, I ran up the mud-slippery path toward the house, then had to swing around and muck back through the dark when Mama called. Papa and Evan had driven on to the barn to unharness and rub down the horses.

Even using the umbrella, Mama and I could hardly see and went slipping and sliding all over. She had a death grip on my arm but was so unsteady she endangered us both. Suddenly, everything struck me as funny—Mama's bonnet all askew, Miss Hallie's wanting to raise Evan, the two of us in the mud. I started laughing and couldn't stop.

Mama caught it from me. "Did you see how your crazy papa drove that team?" she burbled out in my face.

" 'Giddyup, you lazy rascals!' " I mimicked, and we fell on each other's necks, the way Ruth and I might.

Thank goodness for the lantern someone hung on the porch! In such end-of-the-world weather, that flickering light gave Mama and me, rocking like ships, something to steer by.

What we couldn't have anticipated were the good supper smells that met us at the door. Instantly I detected a crisp pork roast and a cinnamony apple dessert. I could see rolls rising on the sideboard.

"Surprise!" cried John, lunging at us from the dining room.

Mary, in Mama's apron, was setting plates around the cherrywood table we rarely used. She greeted us, smiling.

The Rozendals had been butchering when Ted and she stopped by and asked to water their horses. Harley Rozendal had sent a fresh pork shoulder home with them to thank Papa and Ted for their help haying when he'd been down with pleurisy.

The best news for *me* was hearing that Ted was out in the barn doing the milking and would also slop the pigs.

"An' guess who filled the cob box?" John shouted. "Me, myself, and I! Clear to the top."

"Oh, thank you!" I picked him up for a good nuzzling.

I helped Mama with her muddy shoes, then collapsed on a chair and wrenched off my own. When Mary set coffee in front of us, I knew heaven couldn't be any better than what I had right there at home.

If only Evan would stay.

Later, after supper was cleared away, Papa made up a fire in the tall potbelly stove in the dining room—the first fire since April. Naturally, getting it going required some pounding on the flue and no end of grumbling. Mama, extra cheerful after her day in town, turned up the lamp and set it on the shelf. It was Saturday, after all, and the Tuckers' night to play games.

We all watched as Papa cut open a miniature gunnysack and sent two pounds of roasted peanuts rattling across the table. With greedy squeals, John and I scooped up piles for ourselves. Ted brought in a pie tin for shells, Mama sat down, and for a while there was no sound but the blissful cracking and chomping of peanuts.

For some reason that night, we couldn't agree on whether we'd play a board game or a card game. Maybe because Mary was there. With rain still peppering the roof, I was perfectly happy being home near the fire, all of us together, talking and eating peanuts.

Evan finally spoke up to ask if we'd ever played the century game. We'd never heard of it.

"Miss Hallie had us playing it all the time. She claimed it made us think. Taught us history besides."

"History, ugh!" groaned John.

Miss Hallie, ugh! was what I thought. Nonetheless, I kicked John under the table.

"How do we play it?" Papa asked. "Sounds good."

"It's best if we take turns around the table. Each of us makes a prediction about the next century. Could be for 1900, or any time up to 1999. It doesn't matter."

I wondered if thinking about Miss Hallie was making his eyes light up the way they did right then.

"At school we also went a hundred years back— or twenty, or fifty—usually the same as we'd gone forward. We had to tell what was going on then as well. That was the history part." He looked squarely at John. "You know what it means—predictions? We make guesses about the future. We can leave off the history part if you want to."

"Is there a prize?" John wanted to know.

Papa's mustache twitched. "The prize is living long enough to see your predictions come true. Right, Evan?"

"Let's see now," Mama mused, "if that's the case, you and I can't go too far forward, Papa. When the next century ends I'll be 138 years old."

"And in heaven," John added without sadness. "So who's first?"

"You are," I said. "Go ahead."

"Well . . . *I* think . . ." He wriggled around, looked at the ceiling, wriggled some more. *"I* think . . ."

Ted said, "I think you're taking too much time! Let Evan start."

"No, wait, I've got it!" John raised up on his knees, both hands going. "In a hunnerd years people will be so rich, every boy will get a horse and saddle the first day of school. Like getting your reading book. The teacher will say, 'Here's your book, here's your horse an' here's your saddle.' "

"Very good!" Mary praised him.

Mama smiled, and Evan said, "That's the school for me!"

John went on to describe his horse as to age, color, breed and whatnot, until we all shouted, "Enough!"

Papa was next, and I knew what he'd say before he said it. He predicted that William Jennings Bryan would be elected our next president. McKinley would go down in defeat.

"For once," Papa proclaimed with a raised fist, "the farmers in this country will get a fair shake."

A cheer went up. John, in his exuberance, began shouting, "McBryan for president! We want Mc-Bryan!"

Ted laughed and chucked a peanut at him. One came sailing back. When Evan and I started tossing shells, guess who got scolded?

No matter. It was nice to discover Mary was a Populist like us. You can't always be sure. Living as she did at the Scritsmiers' (dyed-in-the-wool Republicans) and having a father who owned a big brickyard in Hastings, she might easily have been of a different persuasion. Papa didn't take to most Republicans.

Mama wasn't quite ready to predict and had to sit and think a minute. The fire behind the yellow squares of isinglass made a pleasant roar. I got up and dumped the tin of overflowing shells into the stove.

"In the next century," she began slowly, as if reciting, "I predict scientists will discover there are good germs as well as bad ones. And the good germs will be . . . unleashed. In vast numbers. And they'll wipe out the bad ones. Someday we'll be free of all these terrible diseases that kill people.

"Is that too wishful for a prediction, Papa?" she asked, having grown pink-cheeked from being the center of attention.

He was thoughtful for a minute. "Um, maybe. You know more about such theories than most people, reading those magazines like you do." Teasingly then, he bent to Mama's face and hoarsely whispered, "A war between germs is no more fanciful than saying we'll go to the moon."

"To the mooooooon!" John shouted. "I wanna see the man in the moon."

But Mama looked a bit crestfallen.

"No, Rachel, I shouldn't make fun." Papa patted her hand. "Why not ask for the moon? We're futurizing, aren't we?"

Ted, at his turn, figured the new century would find all of us driving horseless carriages. "There'll be one in every barn," was his short and sweet prediction. "Wait and see."

118

"Oh, no!" wailed John. "What about Doug and Barney?"

"Off to the glue factory!" quipped Mama.

Papa chuckled and shook his head. "I used to say the same about bicycles, son. It's lots easier riding a wheel somewhere than to feed and saddle a horse. But it didn't happen. Anyway, what would all those devil wagons do for roads? They can't cut through my pasture, scarin' the livestock to death."

Mary leaned forward to tell us Mr. Scritsmier had been hankering for a motorcar the entire summer. "He's been reading about that new Italian 'Feeyat.' Until Mrs. Scritsmier hid his catalogs." She smiled conspiratorially at Mama. "She says they're ugly and smelly and noisy and vows she'll never set foot in one."

Mama nodded, showing she felt the same.

Then Mary went on to predict she'd be wearing a nurse's cap someday. We all stopped munching to exclaim over that. She was already the world's best nurse, in our eyes.

"I don't know when it will be," she said with a glance at Ted, "but someday."

Jumping in ahead of Evan, I predicted we'd someday have a library in Blue Hill—with books to the ceiling. In the *Adams County Democrat* Papa had brought me, I'd read about Andrew Carnegie, richest man alive. All across the land he was building public libraries—for people just like us.

"I'll walk up those smooth stone steps," I said dreamily, "and sit in a nice, soft chair, and read books to my heart's content."

John screwed up his face. "I'd rather have a motorcar!"

"Well, *I* wouldn't!"

"It's Evan's turn," Mama reminded us, but I'd already blurted out, "Hey, I thought of something else!" I drummed my hands on the table, I was so excited. "I predict there'll be machines for milking cows in the twentieth century!"

"Forget it, Cassie," snorted Ted. "You love that job."

Evan finally raised his hand, like at school, in order to get a turn. Everyone laughed, and John reached over and buttoned my lips.

"How about a corn-picking machine?" he said brightly. "Good idea, huh, Ted? We could use one about now." He made a big thing of showing his cracked hands, then allowed John to lean close and inspect the calluses. "I predict there'll be a machine to pick the corn, shell it, toss the cobs in a bin, an' serve breakfast on the side. John, you're gonna have it so easy."

Mary jumped in to say she'd be in seventh heaven over at the Scritsmiers' if there were machines to wash dishes and scrub floors.

"Oh my, yes!" agreed Mama.

I guess it was the image of mechanical hands doing dishes that sent John howling under the table.

"Children, children!" Mama brought us to order. "What do we want with all those machines? Really. What we need is a century of peace. Bring our boys home from the Philippines. They're Ted's age—Bones's and Carl's age—and they're dying over there."

"Amen!" said Papa. "Now that we can blow up everything in sight—thanks to Mr. Du Pont—we can't afford to make war. Now, here's a prediction for you," and he held up a finger. "I foresee that our tired old nineteenth century will go down in history as the bloodiest hundred years known to man."

Who could argue with that? There'd been wars at both ends of the century and the bloody Civil War in the middle.

Such big subjects as war and peace ended our century game for the time being. When Evan opened up a triple, he displayed it in the shell, then, grinning, handed it to John. "There's your prize."

"Ummmmm!" John popped them all in his mouth at once.

Across the table, Ted gave Mary the longest, sweetest look, and then they both started blushing. I figured they were probably holding hands under the table and searched the pile for another triple.

"Papa!" The word exploded from Ted's mouth. "I don't know if it'll happen in this century or the next, but Mary and I want to be man and wife."

My head jerked up.

"And I predict," he continued, gazing at Mary as if for strength, "I predict . . . we'll have your blessing, and will live happily ever after."

"Oh, Ted!" Mama cried. Instantly she was on her

feet, fumbling for a handkerchief. "Marriage isn't a . . . a Saturday-night game! A subject for joking!"

"Rachel," Papa said, "they're not joking. Let them talk."

Mary, given the chance, said, "Ted and I love each other, Mrs. Tucker." The spots brightened on her cheeks. "We want to be wed. We were planning to tell you tonight. We just didn't know how, or when, we'd be able to do it."

"But, Ted, you're so young!" Mama insisted. "How in the world will you support a wife?"

I wanted to yank on Mama's skirt, make her sit down. It wasn't for her to figure out, was it?

"I'll still be farming, Ma. I'm not going anywhere. Harley Rozendal says he's too old for so much land. He wants to put in some durum wheat and hopes I'll farm shares. After seven years, he says he'll sell me the place."

I'd never heard Ted say so much at once, but Mama wasn't budging.

"Papa bought this farm on time," Ted reminded her.

"We're *still* buying it!" she said. "I don't know if it'll ever be paid for, and sometimes it saps the very life out of us!" She wiped her eyes. Her knotted and bent fingers were trembling.

Papa stood, then, and pulled Mama close. His right hand went out to Ted. "Son, Mary, we'll help you all we can. We were young and foolish once ourselves." Kissing the top of Mama's head, he looked at each of us in turn, his eyes shining. "And look what it got us!"

I leaped up, ran around the table, and flung myself at Mary. Laughing happily, we held each other a long time. I didn't care what anyone thought. I had my sister at last!

Mary slept in my bed that night, insisting that Mama not lift a hand, that I was the cleanest and nicest person she'd ever known and that it would be an honor to sleep in my sheets.

I slept on a pallet next to the potbelly stove.

When I put on a serious face and asked if George Washington had ever slept in my bed, Mama herself had to smile.

Chapter 17

Mama called the fall of 1899 "a season of gifts." After the long, parched summer, our mild and sunny fall stretched on and on.

Indian summer came and stayed that last year of the century. Leaves floated to the ground like feathers. Silver-gray sandhill cranes swooped down to feed in the fields—great families of them. Geese honked from their V-formations, and we squinted into the sun trying to count them. Playfully, it seemed, our one and only serious frost turned tumbleweeds into works of art.

Most of the time, John and Evan and I ran off to school without jackets, returning home with sleeves rolled to the elbows. If Evan took it in his heart to let John piggyback on his Indian pony, I'd run alongside and would end up as sweaty as if it were August.

Talking about it later, Mama blamed the delightful weather for lulling us into wrong thinking.

"No, Rachel, it was just plain carelessness!" was how Papa put it. Which meant he was blaming himself.

At church, school—everywhere—people seemed bent on squeezing every pleasure out of "the final days." In town, merchants threw open their doors. CLOTHING OVERSTOCKED DUE TO MILD WEATHER, said signs on storefronts. 1900 DIARIES AND ALMANACS. BE PREPARED! And across the street: TWENTI-ETH-CENTURY STATIONERY HALF PRICE! It was all wonderful, in my opinion.

One Saturday in Blue Hill, Papa let Evan and me off at the dance pavilion, where we watched the young farmers swinging the Bohemian girls. I was intoxicated with the wheezing accordion music and the bright skirts and petticoats that turned girls into whirligigs. I sighed with longing and envy.

"Would you dance with me?" I asked Evan, using the look that sometimes works on Mama. "Pretty please?"

"I would if you were one of those Bohunk girls," he said meanly, and walked off.

When he brought both of us lemonades from a stand at the tent opening, I forgave him. Neither of us knew how to dance, anyway. And Mama mightn't have approved if she'd been there.

Somehow during that glorious month, I stopped

worrying about Miss Hallie. She lived too far away, for one thing. I prayed constantly that she'd marry some rich old guy and forget she wanted to raise a boy. Evan, I'd long since decided, belonged with us.

Another Saturday, the church put on a box social the young men would never forget. Mary got word to the girls in our farm neighborhood that we should decorate our boxes all alike. She then said I should "let the cat out of the bag" when Ted came sneaking around for a hint. Which I did.

"Mary's will be pink and red," I breathed at his ear, "and in a round box, not a square one."

In exchange, Ted did the milking two nights in a row.

Later, when the auction began, nine of the boxes were found to be pink-and-red decorated hat boxes. Ted ended up bidding on Cora Mae's, an old maid twice his age. After losing Cora Mae to Elmer Osguthorpe, he started bidding on mine. When the auction was over, it cost Ted thirty cents to eat with his own dumb sister.

Mary giggled through the rest of the box social, making eyes at him behind her poor fellow's back. Gallantly Ted said my fried chicken was as good as hers. But in the next breath I was hearing, "I'll get you for this, Cassie!"

"Yeah, but just think, you could be over there eating with Mrs. Knightly." Her box turned up pink and red by accident. In the end, she pooled with Queenie, since there weren't enough men to go around. They didn't mind. Papa talked and joshed with them all during supper.

The final caper was the biggest shucking bee ever held in our neck of the woods. The Scritsmiers' yard, strung from one end to the other with paper lanterns, was full of people by noon.

Ruth and I sashayed behind the strolling accordion player, the very one who played for dances in town. John sat gaping at the foot of the juggler, along with the twins and others. The shuckers kept more to themselves, trading jibes and making a show of their muscles. Also, of course, we kids hung around the food and shooed flies.

Long boards—with cloths thrown over—had been laid across sawhorses to provide enough tables. I hoped they wouldn't collapse under so much weight. I'd never seen so many pumpkin pies, such mounds of slaw and potato salad, such a variety of blue-ribbon delicacies: spiced red crabapples, watermelon pickles, deviled eggs. Mmmmmm! Every farm wife had brought her own specialty.

In addition, Mary and Mrs. Scritsmier passed platters of burnt-sugar cookies to keep the youngsters from starving.

In the final round of corn husking, Carl and Ted were pitted against the Jones boys, strapping brothers who were the previous year's champions. As expected, the Jones boys won again, filling the air with husks and boasts. "And enough dust to choke a cow," complained Ruth.

But because Ted found the first red ear of corn, it was he who got to kiss the girl of his choice. We all knew who that would be.

Mama watched poker-faced as Ted, drenched in

sweat, stripped off his gloves and started through the crowd. A moment later he swept Mary off her feet and kissed her soundly, right there in front of the world. A roar went up from the shuckers, then everyone else.

"Will we ever be so lucky?" said Ruth, slapping a hand over her heart and looking moony.

As the days and events propelled us toward year's end, it seemed that nothing but an errant meteor or the Second Coming could come between us and the arrival of the new century.

We were wrong.

"Tragedy never stops to ask permission," remarked Mr. Osgood afterward at school. I never liked the way he drilled me on times tables, but sometimes he was right as rain.

It was the Sunday before Thanksgiving, and we'd done our evening chores early. It was so mild, in fact, we'd turned the cows back out to pasture. Papa had arranged for his old friend Reverend Peabody to fill the pulpit that night. He was to be the capper for Papa's week of revival meetings, so we were expecting a crowd.

"Word's spread far and wide about Ted's healing," I heard Papa tell the Schmidts. "We'll be borrowing benches from the Baptists!"

Ted was already borrowing the buggy so he could pick Mary up in style for the service, which left Mama and Papa with the wagon. They didn't object. Mary had become a real favorite at our house.

Whatever didn't positively need doing that week was put off because of the revival meetings. A brood sow was slated for market, a two-month supply of chicken feed and coal needed to be hauled from town, logs needed splitting, and Queenie had promised to bake the Thanksgiving goose *her* way, with walnut stuffing and currants. She and her family had been invited to our place for the feast, and I could hardly wait.

"But the work of the Lord comes first," Papa said genially. Since it would be my job to stack all that stove-length wood on the porch, I didn't care if we put it off forever.

Sure enough, Sunday had dawned as beautiful as all the previous days. At nine in the morning, a gem-blue sky stretched between horizons like an artist's canvas. By noon, the temperature had soared to sixty.

Inside, the spicy perfume of applesauce canning clung to everything. I loved spending Sunday night at home and was glad when Mama said I could stay behind, if I liked, and see that John got to bed. The service would likely run too late for us, anyway.

We all knew, though no one spoke of it, why Evan wasn't urged to attend meetings with the rest of us.

I made popcorn in a heavy skillet after Mama and Papa left that night, then went back to the book Evan had loaned me from his metal box. I was starting to like the Rover Boys, characters with more spunk than some I found in books.

Evan spent the evening carving soap at the kitchen table, with John watching. We kept a little fire going. Not much, but it made the room cozy.

When the clock struck nine, I was surprised to discover that I'd read thirty-seven pages.

As usual, bedtime meant trips to the privy. We took the lantern and trooped out together, astonished at how much the temperature had dropped.

"Can you smell it, Cassie?" Evan asked as we huddled like moths around the light.

"Smell what?"

"Snow. Hope they've started for home."

I went out again once I was in my flannel nightgown, sniffing the air for a clue. I could see the Milky Way up there. It was going to freeze, all right, but there was no sign of snow. Still, I was glad we'd finally finished the canning. Glad, too, that we'd dug and filled the vegetable pit that week. Mama had insisted on it.

By nine-thirty we were all in bed. I figured it would be eleven before Mama and Papa got home. Later than that for Ted. I went to sleep thinking about the Rover Boys and their high adventures.

The blizzard started sometime before midnight. I mightn't have wakened at all, but the parlor had grown frigid. I remember hearing a *tick-tick-tick* on the windowpanes and waking from a dream. John and I were once again trying to drag shut that heavy chicken coop door.

I pulled up my comforter, snuggled back into my spot, and was gone again in minutes.

Sometime later, I felt John tugging on my covers.

"Cassie, let me in! I'm freezing up there."

I opened the covers and scooted over. John snuggled in against me. Given the nice, unexpected warmth of each other, we were soon asleep again.

By the time I heard Evan walking around—above our heads—it must have been after six. I sat up, wide awake, although I'd been faintly aware that the wind had been howling outside. I listened for kitchen noises. There weren't any, but I could hear Evan's boots on the stairs.

I padded across the cold plank floor to peer out. Snow beat against the panes. I could see little else in the dark, but I figured we wouldn't be going to school in such weather.

"Cassie, come here!" Evan called from the kitchen.

I went in. He was holding a lamp up to the window. I couldn't believe what I saw in that wash of light. The porch was drifted full, right up to the windowsill. Crystal-like tree patterns were already creeping up the panes. We were used to having our windows ice over in the dead of winter, sometimes to an inch thick. But never this fast.

I swung around, thinking to wake Papa. We needed a fire.

"They're not here." Evan carried the light to their room and pushed open the door. I saw the still-smooth coverlet, the empty bed.

Tears stung my eyes.

"They never came home," he said.

Chapter 18

We let John stay asleep. There was no sense in getting him up to a cold house. While Evan went upstairs for his sheepskin coat, I wrapped up in Mama's robe and got a fire going in the cookstove. We'd have oatmeal. I'd make a double batch.

Raking out ashes, I couldn't let myself think about where they were or how they were. We'd heard all the horror stories about the School Children's Blizzard that hit only eleven years before, everyone caught unawares. I'd have to put a lid on my fears about the rest of the family. We were the ones at home and there'd be plenty to do.

I made Evan take time to eat, almost pushed him down on the bench. I poured extra cream and sugar on his oatmeal, sat down to a bowl myself, then asked what in the world we were going to burn if the storm went on. The coal hod for the potbelly stove was empty. The kitchen box was full, but cobs burn fast and would never warm the house in this kind of weather.

Evan didn't answer. His mind was on something else.

Then he was up getting into his coat, pulling on Papa's cap and some wool mittens we'd found in the mothball chest. "I'll have to dig us out first. Any scoops here at the house?"

"I don't think so, unless Papa thought to bring one over from the barn. But Sam'll have the cows in. There's no sense doing anything in the dark. You wouldn't make it as far as the henhouse. Not without a rope. Don't try it, Evan!"

"I'm from Montana, remember?" He opened the door. The wind blasted us with snow and set the curtains flapping. He pushed hard against the screen door, ramming it twice with his shoulder, then ducked back inside. "Go get the coal scoop, would you? I can't more'n budge that screen door. A washpan, too."

"Where do you think you're going?" I asked. "It's terrible out there. You'll get turned around and won't even be able to— Evan, listen to me!"

"No, you listen to me! Even the best dog can't herd cows in a blizzard. Cows'll turn tail to the wind every time. They'll like as not end up at a fence row and stay there. You want to lose your milk cows?"

"If you wait a minute I'll get dressed and help you," I said, back again with what he wanted.

"You will not! Stay inside with John. I won't do anything stupid, Cassie! Keep coffee hot, an' be ready to hand me a lantern when I need it."

I set the lamp on the windowsill and turned it up, then refilled the lantern and trimmed off the blackened wick. I thought of what farms lay between ours and the church—the McIntyres', the Svobodas', the Mays', the sprawling Schmidt place. The Schmidts owned acres and acres and were church members besides. Surely Mama and Papa would stop off there if they had to. But what about Ted and Mary? They were so goggle-eyed about each other, they'd think that white stuff was cotton blowing off the trees. A buggy wasn't much better than a handcart in deep snow.

I could hear John's sleepy voice calling, "Mama? Where is everybody?" I pushed my face up against the icy window. Evan hadn't yet made it to the end of the porch. My stubborn cousin was still throwing snow with a dishpan! I could have helped if he'd let me.

I'd no sooner gotten dressed and set John down for breakfast than Evan was back, stomping his boots and stripping off mittens. He looked like a snowman, right up to his frosted eyebrows. His face was so stiff he couldn't talk at first.

"You ever been in a blizzard before?" John asked Evan, his eyes alight. "I have! Two. Big ones, huh, Cassie?"

Before Evan could answer, I'd thrust coffee into

his hands and pulled scrambled eggs from the warming oven—eggs that disappeared in seconds.

"At this rate," Evan said, "I'll get to the barn by Christmas. Figure as it gets lighter I can reach the woodpile." His cheeks were red, his nose redder. I knew frozen flesh went white, but so far I didn't see any telltale spots.

Evan lit the lantern and said he'd hang it on the hook outside. He warned me again to stay in the house, no matter what.

"It feels close to zero out there," he said as I helped him wind an extra scarf around his face and neck.

John suddenly lifted straight up from his chair. "The chickens!"

I pushed him down again. "They'll think it's still night under all that snow. Really. That's what they do. They go on sleeping."

"But, Cassie, I always feed and water—"

"Not today you don't! Unless it breaks off. When Papa comes home, he'll tell us what we can do."

Evan left then, letting in another barrage of snow.

John scraped up the last of his oatmeal. "What if they don't come home?" he asked.

"They will. Don't worry."

I'd have to find something for him to do.

Daylight finally came, but it made such a weak showing, we joked that someone had turned down the wick. The wind had escalated from howling to shrieking in less than an hour, and I was more worried than ever. In thirty minutes there'd been no sign of Evan. Why hadn't he come back? If he got as far as the chicken coop, he'd surely find the woodpile.

It was a great relief when I opened the door and found a pile of scraggly wood on the porch. It took several trips to bring it in and stack it around the cookstove to dry. I figured he'd gone back for more. But why would it take him so long?

After that I checked the porch again and again. Each time it was harder to force open the screen door against snow that continued to drift. Finally John and I gave up our checker game—we couldn't concentrate anyway—and I got out a pair of Papa's wool pants. I stuffed my dress down inside and pulled on a sweater, Papa's sheepskin coat and a wool hat. John watched until I made him go back to bed to stay warm.

"But Evan said you shouldn't, no matter what!" He waggled a finger at me. "An' you're wearin' men's pants!"

"So? You want me to freeze? Evan won't get back in if we don't keep the porch clear." I chased John into the parlor. "He could be lost out there. What if he's callin' for help and no one hears him? I won't go far, I promise." I pulled the comforter to his chin. "I promise."

Alhough the lantern shed a fair light over the porch, I hardly knew where to start with that dinky little fire shovel.

"Evan!" I called first. In every direction. No answer. Just biting wind and the squeaking of that lantern on the hook.

His tracks were long gone. His "tunnel," as I'd

been thinking of it, looked more like an animal's threshings than a path. I dug and scooped until my back and legs ached and I couldn't feel my fingers anymore, all the while praying that Evan had made it safely to the barn. Out there he might share some warmth with the cows or Papa's new yearling bull. Or with Millie, the only horse left in the barn. He'd be a corpse by now if he was out wandering around.

When I finally gave up, my fingers wouldn't turn the doorknob to get back in. I wrapped my mittens around the lantern to warm my hands, then tried again and got in.

Just in time. John was in bed, all right, but he was crying his head off and the house was like ice. The lamp was sitting on the parlor floor under a window, but it had gone out. Outside one of the panes, spread-eagled as if stuck, was Cawky.

"Oh, John!" I cried.

"I couldn't open the window! And you didn't come!"

"Stay there!" I yelled, and ran across the room.

A lower pane was shattered, and glass littered the floor. John had done his best to reach Cawky, but all he'd accomplished was a big jagged hole through which cold was siphoning into the house.

I ran to get the poker, then finished off the job he'd started, smashing the rest of the pane to its edges. I reached a hand through, closed my fingers around Cawky's cold carcass and pried him loose. His head was encased in a block of ice and he didn't move. Poor bird! He'd frozen to death trying to get in.

John snatched him out of my hands before I could think what to do. Cradling Cawky under his chin, still sobbing hard, he climbed back into my bed and pulled the covers over his head. I let him. He was so sad, and there wasn't a thing to be done.

The state of that desperate crow made me realize what danger we were in. If Evan went snowblind and couldn't guide by the light or find the house or anything, we'd never see him alive again.

I stuffed an entire afghan into the broken window.

Then, hit by an idea, I tore up the steps to Evan's room. I found his rifle in the narrow closet behind his clothes. I'd heard how Florence Rozendal had rung their supper bell for half an hour during the dust storm to guide the farmhands home. We didn't have a bell, but gunshots might serve the same purpose.

I ransacked his satchel and box for cartridges. When I couldn't find any, I realized I'd never even held a Winchester, let alone fired one. I ran my hands over the icy cold barrel. What was I thinking? I might get the heavy thing to my shoulder, but it was no better than Sticky without bullets.

But Evan's wasn't the only gun in the house. I hurried back down to Papa's bedroom. A shotgun would make as loud a noise, and I'd seen him load it enough times. I found the shell box in a dresser drawer.

In haste, I told John what I was doing so he wouldn't be scared when he heard a gun go off. "Stay under that comforter, you hear?"

"Cawky's starting shivering." John sniffled as he continued to stroke the dead bird. "He must've gotten awful cold out there."

Mama would have called it barefaced hope, but I didn't contradict my little brother. My own hopes for Mama and Papa, Ted and Mary, might prove as barefaced as John's.

A minute later I was on the porch with a wool muffler over my ears, the shotgun broken open and loaded—both barrels. I leaned back into the snowdrift so that the kick wouldn't knock me over. It took both thumbs to lift the hammer. Snugging the long gun tight against my shoulder, I aimed at the heavens, let the snow pelt me in the face, and squeezed the first trigger.

The kick pushed me deep into the snowbank, so far in I had to elbow my way out. By the time the sound died, I could swear I was hearing something else. A horse, I thought. A horse whinnying far off, a sound so mixed with wind I couldn't really tell. But I knew it hadn't come from the barn. It had come from the direction of the lane. I had one more shell in the chamber. I lifted the other hammer, braced myself, raised that heavy double barrel and let her go.

No whinnying this time.

After standing the gun against the house, I unhooked the lantern and swung it side to side like a signal. Was it Evan out there? Or someone else? Or no one?

"Mama! Papa!" I screamed. *"Ted? . . . Mary?"* I named them all, but to no avail.

At the far end of the porch, I lunged into snow up to my waist, the lantern over my head. I couldn't see more than an arm's length, but I tried again to follow Evan's path and called until I was hoarse. I listened with all my might for any other sound, but the ferocious wind never let up. It sucked the breath right out of my mouth. I tried to go on, figuring I could find the barn if I kept lining up with the house. But with every threshing step I took, the house grew fainter, until the looming shape behind me disappeared and I was surrounded by dunes of snow.

I had to turn back. There was nothing to guide by. I'd try the shotgun again; then I'd have to give it up. More than anything, suddenly, I wanted to cry. For all I knew, John and I were the only Tuckers left. I couldn't bear the thought of being an orphan. In spite of numb fingers and leaden thumbs, I got off six more volleys before I made myself go in.

John's laughter reached me from the parlor. Cawky's next—his raucous "caw-caaaaw" and his same old earsplitting squawk.

"Cawky!" I rushed in and snatched John's resurrected bird right out of his hands.

"Cawky, honey"—I kissed him on the head—"you came back!"

"I think he was in a coma," John said, spreading his hands like Papa. "When he woke up, it was all at once. Boom! Just like Ted."

We gave each other a good hugging; then I hurried off to build up the fire. As I slung mittens and muffler over a chair back, I was stopped again by the same whinnying sound. But how could I be hearing anything besides the storm? We were buried under drifts. *I must be going blizzard-crazy.* I'd heard of such things.

I broke up some wood and stuffed the pieces in where ashes were still smoldering. I added cobs to get the fire going, wondering where Mama had put the wood ax last spring. I'd soon need it.

I was sweeping up chips when I heard the worst racket on the porch, as if someone were dancing out there. In high-heeled boots! Like *many* someones! The clatter scared Cawky, too. His screams split the air.

I rushed to the door.

"Millie!"

Evan's pony was clean up on the porch, prancing around. I had to push against her nose to get the screen door open. She'd been saddled, and a rope hung from the saddle horn. Her head bobbed up and down and her eyes were wild.

"Where's Evan?" I said—stupidly—before yelling out his name.

Millie kept on nudging me with her nose. I didn't understand her language, but I felt the urgency in it and finally got her out of the way.

I pulled down the lantern and shined it both ways. The feeble light didn't help, and wind threatened to whip it out of my hand. I hooked it back, then worked my way down the steps, trying to follow the boot holes I'd made earlier.

"Stay there, Millie, whoa! Stay right there!"

Evan was in a heap below the steps. He'd collapsed into the same big drift that had cushioned me only minutes before.

"Get up!" I cried, shaking him, trying to lift him. He was caked with snow, his face plastered white. He was also a dead weight. I figured the porch roof had knocked him out of the saddle.

"Come on, Evan, you can't stay here!"

I got up and ran back through the open door, screaming, "John, come quick! It's Evan! Bring the coal scuttle!"

Cold and snow poured into the house, but we propped the screen door open, then set about dragging Evan inside, finally forcing Millie off the porch to do it. Thank goodness Evan came to and was trying to help us by the time we got him to the stove.

John, half frozen himself, kicked shut the door, then went flying upstairs after blankets.

I worked off Evan's hat and muffler. His eyebrows were icy thickets and the leprosy of frostbite dotted his cheeks.

I peeled snow off his face even as he tried to sit up. I'd wrap his hands and feet in turpentine rags, the way we did for a tramp we'd found in the barn.

Once I got him propped against Mama's chair, I opened the oven door for extra heat and got his mittens off. They were curled stiff. He kept trying to talk, but he couldn't.

"Get warm first," I said, the way Mama would. "Then you can—"

I didn't finish because the door no one had bothered to latch suddenly banged open. The blizzard roared into our kitchen like a train. I tried to get up in too big a hurry on that wet floor and went down on my knees.

"Cassie," John shouted, "look there!"

I lifted up to see big old Millie high-stepping in through the kitchen door. She'd upended the coal bucket and was now wedging her huge body through the door frame.

"*Whoooaaa!*" Evan rose up to holler, but she clattered on in, whinnying and showing us the whites of her eyes.

I stood there slack-jawed as she trotted past the table, sideswiped a chair and clopped on into the parlor, where it was roomier.

John squealed with delight. I slammed the door shut and fell against it, wanting desperately to laugh. I knew I shouldn't, knowing if I got Evan started his face would crack like a china doll's. But he couldn't hold back any more than John.

In the end, neither could I.

"Take a little snooze in there while you're at it!" I bellowed after Millie. "Might as well. Everyone else has!"

Chapter 19

It was Queenie—not Millie—who would occupy my famous bed next. She and her family were normally back in Hastings by that time in November, but the fall of 1899, warm weather and the invitation to Thanksgiving dinner had kept them at the river.

There had seemed all the time in the world for Queenie's bunch to return to Hastings, for the kids to begin their parochial schooling and for Queenie to begin her cooking for the Masonic Lodge. Again we were wrong. Mama and Queenie's elaborate Thanksgiving plans were never to be realized.

All through Monday the blizzard continued to rage. It wasn't until early Tuesday morning that the storm finally blew itself out. It was nearly noon, then, before we heard the jangle and clank of harnesses as Mr. Schmidt's horses came trudging up our snow-covered lane. He was bringing Mama and Papa home in his long-bed sledge.

We later learned they'd already deposited half a dozen others at their doorsteps before getting to our house. We also learned that it was Papa with his sharp eyes who had spotted the smoke coming up from the gypsy camp.

Only the few parishioners who had left church before the altar service were thought to have made it to their farms before the blizzard roared in Sunday night. Ted and Mary were two of them. Others—the ones who'd stayed after for coffee and cake—ended up burning the Baptists' benches to keep warm. For years to come, Papa would tell a great loaves-and-fishes story about how they got by.

We three had stories to tell, too, but some parts we kept to ourselves. To get Millie back to the barn before dark, Evan had tied one end of his rope to a porch post, the other to a log in the woodpile. He'd then leaned down from the saddle and planted a row of sticks in the drifts so he could find his way back. Millie wasn't too happy to return to a cold barn, but Sideways Sam—brought back in Evan's arms—was pleased as anything to sleep inside for once. The dog and John kept each other warm.

Evan did tell anyone who'd listen how I'd fired off Papa's big shotgun and saved his life. I wasn't used to so much praise. Each time he told it my cheeks grew warm.

By Tuesday morning a repentant Mother Nature put on such a sunny face, we three walked outside bareheaded. John thought it was great fun peering down *into* the house from the sparkling crust of a drift and then sliding down *into* the barn off the biggest drift of all.

After so much worry, I couldn't stop smiling once I heard, then *saw*, those two teams of powerful Percherons coming up our lane. If Evan had been "something," a UB like me, he'd have been saying, "Thank you, God!"

When we realized it was Mama being unloaded from the sled, the two of us bounded through the snow like deer, coats flapping, to give her a hand. Papa hollered when he saw us coming, then whooped again when he spotted John jumping around on the porch.

But Papa didn't get off when Mama did. He stayed on with Mr. Schmidt while the horses scribed a big circle and headed back the way they'd come.

"Someone's still at the river," Mama said, breathing hard. "I'm very worried!" Then she pulled Evan in close on one side, me on the other. "Oh, my darlings!" I was pretty sure *she* was about to cry. "I was so afraid you'd do something foolish."

"Not us, Mama!" I scolded her. On the sly I was remembering how we'd fed Millie from Mama's oatmeal bin, wiped her down with Mama's towels and kept her in the house for hours and hours. The heat of her big body had warmed the kitchen amazingly.

"But, Mama," I asked quickly, "what about Ted?"

"They're safe at Mary's. Just made it. Word was passed to us as we came along. But, oh, my, the Scritsmiers lost a lot of livestock!"

I looked across at Evan, wondering which of us should tell her about Papa's new bull. Evan had managed to drive the pigs inside the shed during the blizzard, once he'd located the pens. The cows were already safe in the barn, thanks to Sideways Sam, wonder dog. But Evan couldn't find the little yearling bull we hadn't yet bothered to name. In fact, he'd been looking for it when he got lost and had to give Millie her head. Unfortunately, she'd started for the river road, not the barn as he'd hoped.

"She was heading for Montana," Evan joked later.

We'd found the bull, frozen to death.

Tuesday morning Evan had hung and skinned the carcass. He also broke ice in the horse tank and put down feed, while I did the milking and tended to the pigs.

I'd wondered, while doing the chores that day, if we shouldn't have given the pretty Hereford bull a name—General Grant or Paul Bunyan or John Philip Sousa. Maybe he'd have fared better.

Once we got Mama inside, we traded stories, and she patted my shoulder for thinking of the shotgun. Evan's frostbite hadn't amounted to much, but she said turpentine would have worked and was glad I'd thought of it.

John Tell-All, thank goodness, didn't give us away about Millie. Now that he was in school, maybe he was learning more grown-up ways.

Half an hour later, the sled was back from the river. Mama had fixed coffee. Evan had sliced bacon off a half-frozen block and had it sizzling in the pan. We'd have to feed whoever it was, so we'd all rolled up our sleeves. Seeing them coming, Evan put on his coat and went out.

It took the two men, plus Roberto and Evan, to carry Queenie up to the house on an old muskrat coat. Her feet were wrapped in rags, her face smeared and swollen from crying. I'd never seen a strand of her gray-streaked hair out of place until then.

"Queenie!" Mama cried at the door. "What happened? Oh my!" She quickly led them into the parlor, where they laid Queenie down on my bed.

"Raymond . . . my sweet Raymond," she kept moaning. Mama and I pulled up the comforter and tucked it around her. I wanted to stay, but Mama sent me back out to help.

By then Ernestine was handing Marie, the youngest, off the sled to Evan. He carried her through the deep snow to me. Marie's cheeks were feverishly red and she clung to my neck, whimpering.

Evan said, "Your pa says the big kids will go to the Schmidts' after they eat and warm up. Queenie and Marie will stay here."

A lumpy bundle remained at the other end of the sled, away from where the children had been. It was covered with a canvas. I took a deep breath, afraid to ask, but I had to know.

"Where's their papa?" I knew he had a name, but "Queenie's scrawny husband" is what we'd always called him.

Evan pointed to the form on the sled. "Raymond froze to death looking for his horses." He turned me around, then, and made me look him in the eye. "That could have been me, Cassie, if you hadn't fired that gun."

I nodded and went on to the house, carrying Marie. I'd never need more sincere thanks than that.

Chapter 20

Queenie's Raymond wasn't the only one to die in the blizzard. Not far from Spring Ranch, three railroad men pumping a handcar had perished before they could reach the depot. There were others as well, including a couple from across the county line who'd attended the revival meeting. They must have met the blizzard head on. Though they'd wrapped themselves in buffalo lap robes under their overturned buggy, they couldn't stay warm enough to survive.

With no undertaker in Blue Hill and the roads impassable except by sled, the bodies were taken home by neighbors to clean and ready for burial.

Papa rolled up his sleeves and helped Mama prepare Raymond, who spent the night on our dining room table covered with a sheet. He was laid out in a wooden coffin the next day, wearing Ted's outgrown herringbone suit. Everything had to be done quickly because we had no way of embalming him.

The priest couldn't get in from Fairfield, so Queenie, although her family was Catholic, asked Papa to do the service. In the end, he did three at once, with about twenty of us attending. Miss Warwick rode her horse two miles to the church to provide the organ music. It was the day before Thanksgiving.

Queenie wept all the way through "In the Sweet By and By." I wanted to. We hardly knew her Raymond, but I felt great sorrow for her and her brave children and wondered if they'd ever camp on the Little Blue again.

We returned from church in Papa's sled, with Mama and Queenie sitting in dining room chairs tied in so they wouldn't slide. John stood between them, one hand on Mama, the other around Queenie's neck. I sat with Fay and Ernestine, holding Marie, who was wrapped up to her eyes. With the coffin and a few neighbors coming along in a sled behind us, we were a solemn lot.

Ted, Papa, Evan and Roberto carried Queenie—in that same chair—down to the gypsy camp where the burial was to be. They set her down in the black earth that rimmed the grave. Sideways Sam, who'd normally be barking at people he didn't know, curled at Queenie's feet and didn't interrupt Papa once.

A white-faced Roberto stood next to Evan. They knew each other now, having helped dig the grave, using a horse and slip for the worst of it. When Roberto's cap came off for the prayer, so did Evan's.

Around home, things went back to normal once Queenie and Marie were gone. I'd have kept little Marie forever, but the church took up a collection and bought Queenie's family train tickets to Hastings. Papa promised to feed their team over the winter, at no cost whatsoever.

I missed them so. I sighed also for Papa. His salary was never going to be what was promised. There were too many needy people, and he was generous to a fault.

That night Mama and I made up my bed with clean sheets and tried to guess who'd be sleeping there next. I lettered a No Vacancy sign, like I'd seen on Sommerfeld's Boardinghouse, and hung it from a bedpost. Papa said I was getting too clever for him.

Thanksgiving of 1899 was too sad for words. Mama and I did the goose, with the little kids chopping walnuts and Queenie telling us how. So that John and Marie wouldn't be disappointed, we pretended the big meal (one day late) was a true Pilgrim celebration.

It was between Thanksgiving and Christmas that Evan and I had words, when I feared he might just up and leave because of me. Our falling-out started one cold morning on the way to school. John was home with a bad cough, so Evan offered to ride me on Millie. I was thrilled. I'd never ridden her before.

"Do you have your word ready?" I asked at Evan's ear as we bounced along. Our assignment was to bring a new word to school. We had to define it, use it in a sentence, and talk about its history.

"Yep. Two, in case I change my mind. What's yours?"

Now, *heathen* wasn't really my word, but for some reason I wanted to get a rise out of Evan. I don't know why. If it wasn't meanness coming out in me, it was something just as bad.

"And I'll use you for my example," I went on after I'd told him. "I'm gonna say, 'We have a heathen right here in our midst. Evan Tucker. He's not a believer and not a joiner, either.' So, how's that?"

He didn't answer, but, hanging on to him, I felt a tightening in his ribs.

Finally, with a glance back, he said, "You do that, Cassie, and I'm changing my word to *bigot*. You are the perfect example of a bigot!"

"*Bigot!* Never heard that word. You're making it up."

"Look in the dictionary," he shouted into the frosty air.

"No! Tell me what it means."

"It's you, Cassie. Nobody's beliefs are as good as yours. You don't like the foreign-speaking, can't stand Republicans. You're suspicious of Catholics— all except Queenie. You told me so yourself. 'Statues

153

and all that hocus-pocus,' you said. You hate people who're different, and you can barely abide me because I'm not United Brethren like your pa and grandpa. Well, I think for myself. If you want to call me names, go ahead, but *bigot* won't be one of 'em."

"I was only joshing," I said lamely. My face burned. My real word was *interment*. I don't know why I didn't tell him.

He let me ride Millie home by myself that day—if I'd promise to curry her afterward. He said he wanted to walk with Janie Marsh, but I think he was trying to make it up to me. I figured I could never make things up to him.

It was mid-December before Papa and Ted could get to Blue Hill for a load of coal. The rest of us stayed behind to tame the woodpile. We complained loudly among ourselves, but in the end made it fun by having silly prizes, then fixing it so John won them all.

That same day Papa brought home Miss Hallie's letter. Evan went directly upstairs to read it, and all my old worries flooded in. I was full of regrets. Why had I called him a heathen? I'd be mad at God, too, if I'd lost everyone in my family. Evan was one of the nicest, kindest people I knew. And *bigot*, I'd decided after looking it up, was about the ugliest word in the English language.

The rest of us hung around downstairs, waiting uneasily for Evan to come back down. Mama made a pot of coffee, and John sort of fretted. We all knew Evan Tucker was Miss Hallie's star pupil and that she earnestly wanted a hand in his education.

"Well?" Papa asked when he joined us again.

Evan grinned at John. Me next. I guess he could read our faces. Then, as if wildly relieved, he tossed the letter over his head and let it plummet to the floor. "She's taking a job in Denver and won't be through after all. Her lawyer said being guardian is a risky business with me so far away. Unless I want to live there—"

John ran up and grabbed him around the waist. "You're staying with us, you!"

Evan grabbed him back and mussed his hair. "Heck, I was too independent to be someone's ward when I left there."

Ted clapped him on the back, and Mama and Papa broke into smiles.

"Hey, Cassie!" Evan said, scooping the letter up from the floor. "Look how it was addressed." He handed it to me, grinning, and I read it aloud:

Mr. Evan Tucker
c/o Cassie Tucker
Blue Hill, Nebraska

"In care of *me*? Why'd she do it that way?"

"I told her about you, for one thing. She said I'd be in good hands with a spunky cousin like you."

"She did?" I took back all the mean thoughts I'd had about her.

"Anyway," he went on, "she wants me to keep writing so she knows how I'm doing."

He swung around and gave John a couple of punches. "Enjoy teaching in Denver, Miss Hallie. I'm doin' just fine where I am!"

Chapter 21

Christmas that year was the most memorable of my childhood. Not because it snowed again (it didn't) or because there were parties (there were none) or because we gave each other elaborate gifts (they were mostly homemade). It was special because we were all together. And because I knew, as we left the nineteenth century behind, that there'd never be another Christmas quite like it.

I spent much of the day reading *Heidi*, which Evan had bought in Blue Hill without my knowing. John spent the day learning soap carving with a pearl-handled knife I'd seen among Evan's treasures. Ted and Mary spent the day doing everyone else's chores, as they'd promised on notes pinned to oranges in our Christmas stockings.

Our prayers that night began and ended simply: "Lord God in Heaven!" Papa said, bellowing it out, making a joyful proclamation of the four words. "We have so much to be thankful for!"

And we did. Ted had returned to health. Evan had endured. Cawky came back, as John told us often enough. And Mama's rheumatism actually got better, she said, with all the excitement.

It was a good thing Papa never got around to building my screen. Mama used the flowered chintz for a new Christmas dress for me, seeing as how we weren't going to need that screen. Ted and Mary would wed in March before planting began. Afterward, Papa would begin the addition to the house—a room for Ted and Mary. Evan and John would then have Ted's old room, which meant I'd be back upstairs where I belonged. I was *ecstatic*! (Ruth's word on vocabulary day.)

In truth, I had only one worry as the clock ticked off the last hours of the nineteenth century. Would Evan go with us to the New Year's Eve service?

It was our family's tradition to see the New Year in on our knees. At church. I tried to explain the "gathering for prayer instead of revelry" part to Evan and why it was called the Watch Night service. I was surprised he'd never heard of such a thing. This year, Papa had renamed it the Century Watch and had been preaching about its meaning for a month.

I'd also told Evan how Papa always strung sleigh

bells over Doug and Barney, and how, with Mary along, we'd be sure to have singing. We'd rock along under the stars, all snuggly under blankets and robes, a lantern lighting the way.

I must have convinced him. When we all assembled to go, here came Evan down the stairs wearing his Blue Hill suit, his father's sheepskin, and the muskrat hat Ted and Mary had given him for Christmas. For her part, Mama was wearing the brooch Evan had brought from Montana and given her as a Christmas gift. It looked beautiful on her black Sunday dress.

Later, from his place at the pulpit, Papa took out his vest-pocket watch and said we should prepare now to see the old century out, the new century in. It was five minutes to midnight, and I could feel goose bumps rising on my arms. John reached over for my hand. I think he still expected the world to end and wanted someone to hang on to.

Papa had us close our eyes to make resolutions first. Mine were easy. I'd root out all the bigotry from my heart, thereby learning to think for myself. I'd also try harder at arithmetic so that Mr. Osgood would let me read what I pleased.

Then everyone knelt for prayer.

"You don't have to pray if you don't want to," I whispered to Evan, my palms suddenly sweaty.

"It won't hurt me," he whispered back.

So I knelt down between John and my cousin and closed my eyes.

When Papa's midnight prayer ended and I looked up, Evan was gone.

My heart sank, but not for long because the bell in the tower was ringing and ringing—a deep *gong, gong, gong*—and everyone was shouting out "God bless!" and "Happy New Year!" and "Happy twentieth century!" Papa bounded down from the platform to give us all hugs and to pump Ted's hand.

"Where's Evan?" John asked, looking around, even under the pew.

Papa laughed. "Who do you think that is ringing the bell?"

Mama threw me a wink. Papa and Mama had arranged it all beforehand. I knew why, and it made me love them all the more.

John fell asleep going home. Ted and Mary sat close, her head on his shoulder. Try as I might, I couldn't hear a word they said.

That left Evan and me on our backs, gazing up at the black dome of sky and its million pinpricks of light. He told me how Papa, after reading Miss Hallie's letter, had promised to send him to Fairfield for high school the next year. Even if he had to sell a calf to do it.

"I'd be boarding out somewhere," Evan said, "so I'd have to leave Millie behind. Think you could take care of her for me?"

"Oh, Evan, I'd take such good care of her!"

"You'd have to ride her to school most days. You and John. I'll come home"—and he'd used the word *home*—"for holidays and to help farm in the summers, so I don't expect she'll forget me."

I didn't care if it was unseemly. I flung my arms

160

around Evan and squeezed the breath out of him. I didn't mind being second in his affections to Millie. I knew exactly how he felt.

"I don't really think you're a bigot," he said sheepishly after I let him go.

"I'm not," I replied. "Not anymore."

I pulled the itchy lap robe to my chin and craned around to get my bearings by the Big Dipper, marveling that the new century didn't feel any different from the old. But that was how Papa had said it would be. With change on every hand, it was a comfort to know the seasons and centuries would cycle on and on, the way they were supposed to.

"Dear Diary," I'd write when I got home. "My name is Cassandra Evangeline Tucker. Today is the first day of the twentieth century and I'm about to turn twelve. What could be better?"

Afterword

The phrase commonly used to describe the years from 1890 to 1900 is *the gay nineties*. That rosy description might have come close to fitting life in the bustling gaslit cities where tycoons were making fortunes in steel and railroads, and where the wealthy sailed off for long European holidays, their seventeen steamer trunks borne by porters. But for most Midwestern farm families, the last ten years of that century were anything but carefree.

Take the weather. Cassie's family was used to extreme weather—twisters that plucked feathers off chickens, hailstones that chopped gardens into vegetable salad, blizzards that could endanger life in a matter of minutes.

But droughts! Droughts came and stayed. The one beginning in 1893 stretched on to 1897. Crops failed for four years running. Unable to pay more than the interest on their mortgages, farmers went scurrying back to Iowa and points East—whole wagon trains of them. The Adams County population dropped from 24,303 in 1890 to 18,840 in 1900. Banks that hadn't already failed took over the farms rapidly. Rachel Tucker had good reason for bitterness when she reminded Ted that the farm "sometimes saps the very life out of us."

Railroads, too, fell on hard times when there were no hogs, chickens or cattle to ship East. The owners tore down roundhouses and closed lines, leaving tracks to rust. Workers were laid off by the hundreds.

One family in a small Nebraska town remembered having nothing to eat during the winter of '94 but cornmeal mush and turnips. Even so, they shared what they had, neighborliness being next to Godliness in that day and age.

Add to troubled economic times the constant threat of disease. One epidemic after another swept across the plains states, sometimes wiping out several members of a single family. The children's diseases—whooping cough, the measles, "summer complaint"—struck rich and poor alike. Suicides and house-burnings increased. Overcome by tragic losses, any number of people simply gave up their sanity. Such grim years would be enough to "dethrone one's reason," a phrase commonly used during the "gay" 1890s.

By 1898, prosperity began to return to south-central Nebraska. The rains came back. Crops flourished. The Populist party rose up to champion William Jennings Bryan, "the Great Commoner." As Teddy Roosevelt galloped onto the national scene, America was flexing its military muscles in faraway South Africa and the Philippines. National pride and optimism were on the rise. Although doomsayers noisily predicted the world's end, the Tuckers fell under the spell of new-century optimism and all that a seemingly golden future promised.

By 1899, when Cassie's story begins, vast networks of railroads connected prairie towns to cities. Nonetheless, twenty-five hundred autos were produced that year—with scarcely ten miles of concrete roads in the country to serve them.

Nearly nineteen thousand people were employed across the land as telephone operators. One home in seven had a bathtub, and electric streetlights were popping up in the most improbable places. Boston, that year, led all other American cities in replacing its horse-drawn trolleys with electric streetcars.

In tiny Nebraska towns like Broken Bow and Blue Hill, families gathered in churches to hear Thomas Edison's amazing "talking machine," which featured a cat fight real enough to confound listeners. And, thanks to the sped-up spreading of news, even country folks were aware of what was new and fashionable. They, too, wore Levi's pants, served Jell-O gelatin, drank root beer, and played whist. The first Coca-Cola was bottled that year, ragtime became the latest musical fad, and Willa Cather, who would become Nebraska's best-known writer, saw her first work published in magazines.

"So many advances!" Cassie might have said. "Enough to give a person goose bumps on top of goose bumps!"

When the commissioner of patents, Charles H. Duell, said in 1899, "Everything that can be invented has been invented," he was surely mouthing the optimism of the day. Already people had put the grim decade of the nineties behind them.

But history tends to repeat itself. Thirty years after the date of Cassie's first diary entry, my maternal grandparents lost their Nebraska farm near the Little Blue River. Hard times returned tenfold. Farmers suffered even more extremes of drought and heat, even worse dust storms. Untold numbers were uprooted as a result. The drought of the 1890s now seemed a mere rehearsal for the terrible years of the 1930s. In truth, as Rachel Tucker put it to her children, "Nebraska was never intended for the faint of heart."

Today, cruising along I-80, visitors think of Nebraska as the state that takes too long to cross. Perhaps they should leave the freeways and check out the dusty back roads. Eat *runzas* and pie in the little cafés. Talk to the old-timers. Nebraska—a melting pot of nationalities and faiths—is, to this day, known as a friendly, helpful place. One hopes the neighborliness that pulled Evan and Cassie, Ted and Queenie through their crises is as much valued now as it was at the turn of that *other* century, the nineteenth.

About the Author

Ivy Ruckman on *In Care of Cassie Tucker:*

"Can you imagine cramming a family of seven into a two-room sod house? As a college music student and young teacher, my grandmother must have had other plans for herself. But choosing to be a frontier preacher's wife meant choosing a life of hardships as well. By age thirty, living so primitively, she was crippled by arthritis in her hands and feet. Even so, she nursed her family through typhoid fever, broken bones and—in my father's case—a life-threatening coma. That tough resourcefulness persisted into her late eighties, when, in spite of daily pain, she stitched heirloom quilts for every one of her twenty-four grandchildren.

"I like to think Cassie Tucker is carrying my grandparents' genes in this fictional account of a farm family's life in 1899. Inspired by the memoirs of two remarkable aunts, Eva Hein and Hallie Nelson, I found revisiting my own Nebraska roots a rewarding adventure."

Ivy Ruckman is the award-winning author of fourteen novels for young readers, including *Night of the Twisters* and *No Way Out.* She lives in Salt Lake City and St. George, Utah, where on winter mornings she climbs to the top of a hill to see the sun come up. She has three grown children who love books as much as she does.